Walking Through Hell
A Natural Experience

LaCinta Brown

(paperback) ISBN: 978-1-955605-15-1

For more information:
Email: overcomerceo44@gmail.com

Printed in the United States of America

Also, By LaCinta Brown
Oh, It's Okay

Table of Contents

Excerpt from *Oh, It's Okay*

Damon began to get bad vibes from the neighborhood we lived in and started looking for another house. Months later he found a house and we moved in. Things seem to be getting back on track. Damon had come in the house around 10:30 pm one night. His eyes were beet red from drinking. "Kim, put this fifteen thousand up." Damon said. "Okay!" I responded. I began to count it. "Damon, I need five hundred for some bills." Damon became enraged. "Bitch are you stealing from me?" he insinuated. "No, I'm not!" I yelled standing to my feet. Damon walked out of the bedroom and grabbed his shotgun and put it to my head while I bent over picking up the money.

"No, Jesus, Jesus!" I cried.

At that moment, all I knew was to call on Jesus. I had no one to handle Damon without blood being shed. I kept my eyes closed and called on Jesus repeatedly. At that moment I knew my marriage was over.

Damon threw the gun down, ran over to me and held me while apologizing. "I'm sorry, I blacked out!"

Damon cried trying to convince me he didn't do intentionally.

"No, Damon, let me go!" I yelled.

"You had a gun to my head. What is wrong with you?"

I demanded to know looking at Damon waiting for an answer.

"All I've ever around are people trying to get my money. I thought you was taking money from me." Damon said with a frowned-up face.

"Since it's extra money I figure I could go ahead and pay a couple of bills." I explained.

"No, we will pay it when its due." Damon said walking out the room with the gun in his hand.

"No, you can pay it. I'm not staying here after you put a gun to my head." Damon said something smart.

"I ain't no killer but don't push me!" I yelled out of nowhere pulling my gun out, shooting it and purposely missing him.

"Why did you shoot at me? Bitch I'll kill you!" Damon said biting on his bottom lip.

"The same reason you put a shot gun to my head. I blacked out!" I hollered back.

"Kim, give me my motherfucking money!" Damon said walking towards me.

"Your best bet is to walk on the other side of the bed and pick the money up," I said harshly.

Damon raised his hand as if he were attempting to grab the gun. I shot him in the shoulder. He flew back a bit but didn't fall. Now Damon was beyond mad.

"It's on the bed, get it, and stay away from me!" I yelled pointing at the money with the gun in my hand and staring Damon in his eyes.

"Come closer I'll kill you!" I told Damon.

Damon touched his shoulder and blood was pouring out. He snatched a shirt from the closet and wrapped it around his shoulder. He then picked the money up and walked out of the room.

I grabbed my luggage and began packing everything in my view. "Where are you going?" Damon asked.

"I'm leaving, I can't stay here with you putting a shot gun to my head!" I said steadily packing.

"You don't have to leave. I'll leave shit! You shot at me, then shot me, and now you want to leave," Damon said while holding his shoulder that started having a burning sensation.

"You need to go check on your shoulder. Then stay gone for a while, not just one night."

"Kim, I don't want us to be away from each other. I'm sorry, I blacked out," Damon said.

"I don't know if I'm going to be here when you get back," I told him.

Damon stayed out of my sight. However, I knew he had been home because he left his clothes on the floor and hospital discharge paperwork was on the dresser. Since he won't stay away, I'll leave. I grabbed my Fendi luggage along with my duffle bag filled with my personal stash and left.

Chapter One

Kim
One week later

Since being married to Damon, the last three years had been hell. I have experienced enough hurt and disappointment for a lifetime. I had been longing to get away from him. The last thing I wanted to do was neglect the vows I made before the Lord. All the arguing over nothing and the verbal abuse was taking a toll on my mental and physical health. Being called bitches all the time was not sitting well with me. No matter how bad things got. I tried to stick it out. One thing was for sure if ever hit me he would be dead.

Thank the Lord our children were with my mother. Realizing my decisions were not always the right decisions. I begin to cry. Not only are my children affected by our decisions but his children are as well. His children and I had developed a wonderful relationship. Daphne had started to come over more by choice. Sometimes I felt Denise was trying to bring a wedge between our relationship. Instead of fighting and arguing I allowed Damon to handle to her. Eventually, Daphne was with us every weekend, holidays also while on school breaks.

Being the middle end of October, the weather was around sixty during the day and cold at night. The night I left Damon I had no idea where I would go. I didn't know if I will get a room or where to go. Then I remembered my house was tenant free. After my last tenant moved out the house. I decided to put it up for sale. I had it staged, but quickly changed my mind after several bad situations at home. I sold majority of the furniture and kept the bedroom suit. I pulled into the driveway, turned the engine off, opened the back door of my truck I grabbed my bags and closed the door heading to the front door of the house. Unlocking the door, I hit the switch to turn on the lights. Dorn it, only one light came on from the light fixture. Walking to the back bedroom I felt around on the wall for the remote holder. Grabbing the remote I turned the light on and tossed my purse in the chair sitting bags down by the chair and took my shoes off. Being mentally drained I ran some bath water to help take my mind off my martial issues. Getting everything together for my bath. I broke down crying. How could my husband put a gun to my head? I asked myself. After bathing I got in the bed and fell asleep. The next morning. I woke up in a better mood. I dressed in pair of blue distressed jeans, a black fitted sweater, a pair of black knee-high boots with black diamond accessories. I open the door hit the remote start on my truck so it could warm up. Thirty minutes later, I hoped my truck headed to get a message. My body had been under some stress lately and I noticed my bones were starting to protrude out my back. Making my way into the spa I noticed some of Damon's fans. All these hoes do is hee-hee. I rubbed my left hand over my face blinded them with my wedding ring and they quickly shut up. I am a little petty especially when it comes to people who don't like me. Find a validate reason not to like me. You wanting a married man is your problem not mine. I checked in and was immediately taken back. Getting undressed I laid on the massage table and rested my mind.

Feeling better. I called my hair stylist to see if he could me in today. Today was my lucky day someone cancelled their appointment and I was able to get right in. Parking in front of the salon I walked inside. "Hey Kim!" AJ said walking towards me giving me hug. "Hi AJ!" What are we doing today? He asked as I sat down in his chair. He turned me to face the mirror and massaged my scalp. "You can straighten it!" "What's going on with you?" He asked in a caring manner. "The same thing, me trying to figure out my life." I said mentally internalizing what I said. At that moment I realized I was living my life for others. I don't want to be in a violent, verbally abusive relationship. I want my husband to cherish me, build me up, love on me. "Go after your dreams, what is it that you really want?" he said interrupting my thoughts. Instead of responding at that moment. I let that ponder while he cleansed my scalp and hair. Walking back to the chair I heard my phone ring. Looking down at Damon calling I ignored his call by hitting the silent button.

"It's time for me to finish my business degree. I started working on during the first year of our marriage. Things became hectic, my grades started slipping. After that semester I didn't sign up for more classes." I responded as he was detangling my hair. "You need some finishing power. Start speaking what you want and go for it. Whatever is going in your personal life is a distraction and you must ignore it. The enemy is going to keep coming at you because you will always fight the person, forgetting it's a spirit." He said putting the brush down and leading me to the hair dryer. Everything he said was true. The bible says" for we wrestle not against flesh and blood, but principalities, against powers, against the rulers of the darkness of this world, against spiritual wickedness in high places. Ephesians 6:12 KJV

Sitting under the hair dryer my phone rang again.

Becoming annoyed I quickly answered the phone. "Damon, I am under the hair dryer. I will call you back later." I said then disconnected the call.

After an hour of me sitting under the dryer my hair was completely dry. AJ motioned for me to come to the chair. Sitting silently his chair I thought how nice it would be to have a loving marriage. Looking in the mirror and shaking my head I was satisfied with my look. Paying AJ, we hugged said our goodbyes and I headed to my truck.

As soon as I started the engine my phone rang again. Answering through the Bluetooth.

"Yes, Damon" I answered.

"I want you to come have dinner with me." He said kindly.

"Damon I am not coming home in your current mental state. You have been irrational. I think you should get counseling." I said rolling my eyes.

"I'm missing my family that's all." Damon explained.

"You should have thought about that before you put the gun to my head. You overreact to everything. There was no reason for you to put a gun to my head. Sometimes I wish I would have walked away from you at the altar." I said everything that came to mind.

"You are a nothing ass bitch." He yelled.

But the truth was I no longer cared what he thought about me. I disconnected the call and sat back in the seat while my mind started to relive the last three years of my life. What are you doing I asked myself out loud? I snapped out that quick. We are not thinking backwards. Forward thinking only!

Making it a one stop shop I headed to Walmart. I grabbed a cart from inside the store. Loading my cart with goodies. I paid for the items and exited the store. While loading the groceries in the truck. My phone began to ring. Allowing my phone to ring I Ignored the call. Starting the engine and getting comfortable in the seat I pushed the heated seat button. Making my way back to the house the phone rang again. Answering through Bluetooth gave a delay.

"What's taking you so long to answer your phone?" Damon asked in an aggressive manner.

"What is that you want?" I asked in a fed-up voice.

"It's 9 o'clock! What time will you be home?" Damon asked sounding frustrated.

"I moved out. What part of that are you not getting? You said you would stay away but you haven't held your part of agreement, so I left."

"Stop the bullshit, Kim. I had to come by to check on the house make sure everything is alright. I'm not going to leave my family out here alone," Damon voiced in aggravated manner.

"You could have called to check on us just like now. I am not in the mood to discuss this, and you have been drinking. Call me tomorrow and we can finish this conversation." I said and disconnected the call.

Pulling in my driveway seeing Damon 745 BMW had me hot! I wanted to backout the driveway and drive until I couldn't drive anymore.

Paying him no attention. I got out the truck, unlocked my front door. I made several trips to truck before all the groceries were inside the house. Attempting to close the door. Damon walked in sloppy drunk.

"What Damon, what do you want? I asked in calm voice.

"Come home. I asked you earlier to have dinner with me. You can't stay here. Look around, you don't have any furniture." He spoke.

"I have furniture coming the middle of the week." I said with my hand inside my purse holding my gun.

"I didn't come over to fight with you, I want my family back that's all."

"You are mean and dangerous I will not live my life with whatever issues you will not to deal with them."

"As of right now we are separated and you are free to do whatever you like with whoever you like. I'll be filling for a divorce soon." I said opening the door for him to leave.

He laughed Devashish saying" we are not divorcing then walked out the door leaving it open. I quickly closed it. The way he said had me shook. Now I feel like I am living a real-life nightmare.

I put my things away leaving out the items I planned to cook. Pulling out my pan I warmed it add butter then fried my shrimp. Fixed a side salad with dinner rolls. I poured a shot of Hennessey. Eating my food in silence is not what I needed. "I should have got me tv from Walmart." I said out loud. I cleaned the kitchen and started my bath water. Sitting in the tub I thought about what to do next. After Damon I married. I convinced him to combine Anderson Luxury Motorcycles and Anderson Body Service in the same building where I took over the day-to-day operations. So foolish of me not to have a backup plan. Should I stay where I am or should I look for something else? I knew from the beginning this marriage was not going to work. Now here I am living separate from my husband trying to figure how to tell the children this is our new home. Hearing my phone notifying me of a message I picked up. Looking at the phone it was 10:45 pm. Opening the message. **Damon; Come home.** Deciding to ignore him I got in my bed said a prayer turned the lights off and dozed off.

Sitting up in my bed gathering my thoughts from the dream I had.

"Lord please keep me from all hurt, harm, dangers seen and unseen."

Laying back down the alarm went off at 6 am waking me. Getting my blue tooth speaker from my bag I connected it to my phone and played *Mary Mary's I survived.* Unsure of how the day was going to go I dressed in a pair of black Levi jeans, black fitted multi color sweater and a pair of black booties. Standing in the mirror I pulled my hair in a low ponytail and place diamond studs' earrings in my ear. Hearing my phone ring I walked over to the nightstand on the side of the bed to pick the phone up and answered.

"Hello"

"I need you to come to work today. I have somethings I need to take care of out of town I'll be back in a couple days." Damon said.

Allowing his words to permeate, I wanted to know who he was going with, but at the same time I really don't care. Saying "okay" I disconnected the call relieved we didn't disagree about anything. It had been two weeks since I had shown up to work. Damon could run the shop but his patience was too thin to deal with customer service issues.

I finally arrived parking my BMW in back I hopped out being met by the security guard on duty.

"Good morning Mrs. Anderson." Bruce the security guard said walking me to the door.

"Good morning." I responded back with a smile on my face.

Since Damon handed me the reigns. Business has increased. Financing became available but majority of sales were cash. One night leaving the shop a guy attempted to rob Damon but that didn't end well. A cop was driving around and noticed the situation intervened quickly. Since then, Damon always had armed security on the premises when I was there. Whether he was there or not.

Unlocking the door, I turned the alarm off quickly then walked to my office. Opening the door, I noticed a bouquet of red and white fresh roses sitting in the center of my oakwood desk with a note attached to it. **I love you! Damon.** I opened my closet to put my purse away it was more roses. I smiled put everything away. Hearing the phone ring I walked back to front of Service Center.

"Thank you for calling Anderson's, how may I help you?" I answered the ringing phone.

"I take it you got the flowers by the smile on your face." Damon asked.

"I did get the roses. Thank you very much for the gesture." I spoke.

"You're welcome, come home!"

"Why, aren't you leaving town for a couple of days? We need martial counseling first." I continued.

"Let me focus on the road." Damon said and disconnected the call.

Getting comfortable behind my desk I unlocked my desktop to look over the work orders. Before I knew it 7:45 am was here and the workers started to fill in the place. Hearing the machines going I got up to inform everyone I would be in my office if they needed anything. I walked back to my office and closed the door. Sitting in my cream-colored leather chair. I picked up the vase up and smelled the roses. Smelling the rose I started to daydream about my next move but that was interrupted by a knock on the door.

"Come in" I said with a raise voice.

Amelia comes strutting in with a pair of pair of wheat-colored leggings with a long-colored thigh high sweater, Jimmy Choo Crystal Timberland boots with crystal accessories.

"Hey" Amelia I said getting up from behind my desk walking towards her.

"Oh! I love your swag with those boots!"

"Have a seat," I said walking towards my sofa.

"Thanks girl!"

Amelia responded taking a seat on my cream leather sofa.

"What brings you by?" I asked sitting on the edge of sofa.

"I am on my way to Lisa's to get a fill-in and came by to see if you wanted to go!" Looking at my nails.

"I just got them done a couple of days ago and Damon left to go on a trip this morning!"

"A trip and you stayed behind intentionally?" She questioned with a raised eyebrow.

"Someone has to stay behind to run the business." I responded not letting her no Damon and I were separated.

Anyone who knows me, knows traveling is what I live for.

"Bump is leaving for San Diego tomorrow for a couple of days. He did mention it was a business trip." She added looking at her Frost Rolex.

Getting up front the couch "Kim, I am going to head to the shop!"

"Thanks for stopping by" I cooed as I stood up to walk up the front."

"Make an appt for me in a couple of weeks. My nail tech moved away and I have trying different shops but I have not found one I am committed too." We said our goodbyes and I went back in my office.

Looking at my children's picture on my desk I begin missing them more but glad they are at my mother's for fall break. With everything going on I am not sure how the children will react when they find out Damon and I are separated. Hopefully, Damon and I could sit down and have an adult conversation about co-parenting. Lately I have been enjoying my peace. When I am around him, it's so much tension. His mood changes with liquor in his system making everything worse.

Every time I think of him or say his name he calls.

"Hello." I answered.

"How did things go today?" Damon asked.

We talked for a little longer then ended the conversation. I had to get home and prepare to file for my divorce the next day. I was glad my rental house was empty. I backed in the driveway and got out. I opened the door, walked to my bedroom, and placed my purse down on the bed. I got my laptop out searching for divorce lawyers. This is harder than I thought. Damon came across my mind. I called his phone to discuss business matters only for him to say something about some underwear. I was hoping he would say he was with someone else. I would let him go without a fight. Instead, he lied. I disconnected the call for him. Trying not jump to conclusions. I told myself. I'll see how this play out. I went back searching for a lawyer writing a couple more of them down. I closed my laptop. I got out my bible and read for a little while before taking a shower and calling it a night.

Now that the children are back the house was full of life. My furniture was delivered last week. The children's rooms were put together. Onya room has white walls, pink, and purple curtains with bedding to match. All the children have brown wood furniture. The boys room has blue walls with brown and blue curtains. Everyone seemed excited about the rooms. Surprised no one asked about the change. Daniel is now three, Jr. is thirteen and Onya is fifteen.

"Tell me about the trip" I said with excitement.

"Jr. got in trouble because he kept talking back. Onya was talking on the phone to her boyfriend and what did you do Daniel?" I asked laughing.

"Being a tale tell like now", Jr. said.

"Shut up Jr." she asked me and punched Jr. in the face.

"No, stop Daniel please don't start."

Hearing the doorbell ring. I made my way to the door and noticed it was Damon. I opened the door and walked away without speaking. The children came out their rooms. I went to my room and closed the door. About two hours later Damon came busting in my room without knocking on my door.

"Can I help you sir?" I asked while searching for schools to finish my degree.

"You just going keep me from my family?" Damon asked taking a seat on bench at the foot of my bed.

"I haven't kept you from your family. You been laughing and having a good time with them in the living room. You can take them if you want too."

I said not looking at him.

"Alright, you want to play games lets' play." He stated.

Walking back towards the living he told the boys to pack their things for the weekend. I went to pack Daniel's things. On the way to his room Damon grabbed me attempted to kiss me, but I turned my head. He let me go.

"Come on Daniel and Jr. let's go." Damon called out to boys walking towards the front door.

Once they were gone.

"Onya let's go shopping." I yelled from my room.

I allowed the truck to warm up while we got dressed. The temperature had dropped tremendously.

"Hold on, I have to grab a warmer coat." I told Onya as I unlocked the truck for Onya went back inside and switched coats.

"Where are we going?" Onya asked.

"Walmart so I can start Christmas shopping."

"Oh, we're going window shopping! I should stay home! "Onya said cracking up making me laugh as well.

"What happened for us to move back to the old house?" Onya asked.

We weren't seeing eye to eye so I felt it was best if I moved out.

"Have you decided what your major going to be?" I asked changing the subject.

"Yes, I have, Psychology" She said proudly.

"Excellent choice." I second her decision.

Finding a parking spot at Walmart was like searching for needle in a haystack. Someone backed out and I pulled right in. We got out and headed inside.

"Grab a cart Onya" I told her as she was walking inside.

Walking through the toy isle in the boy section I grabbed whatever I thought Daniel would play with that he did not already have.

"Momma Daniel will not play with them toys buy him a game system and a couple of toys." Onya said removing some of the toys from the basket.

We walked through Walmart finding things I could use for the house. We made it to the check out. I smelled an intoxicating scent. I looked at the guy wanting to know the name of the cologne but I was stuck. My mouth would not open. This man had smooth coco skin, freshly trimmed beard, fresh fade with hazel eyes. He wore a camel- colored pea coat with the collar raised.

"Hello", he said in a baritone voice looking into my basket.

"Hi" I responded I said putting my things on the conveyor belt.

Going into his pocket he pulled out his card and handed it to me.

"Attorney Monty Stapleton." I said out loud.

With him standing facing me I noticed he was dressed in Balmain jeans, Balmain shirt and pair of Jordan's I would have never thought he would be an attorney. Onya cleared her throat.

"I'm sorry sir she's married." Onya said.

"I apologize I don't see a ring on her finger." He said gathering his things up.

"Yes, Monty I'm married I just don't wear a ring." I said looking at my bare hand.

Maybe, one day I will see you with an inner smile he stated and walked off. I could feel Onya staring at me ignoring her I heard the cashier say $467.85. I paid for the items and Onya placed them in the cart and walked to the car. We stopped at Red Lobster and order some to go crab legs and lobster tail.

Pulling into the driveway. We grabbed the bags and raced in the house to get out the cold. We put everything away and hid Daniels toys. Getting comfortable in my bed I pulled out Monty card. What are you doing? I asked myself. Hearing a knock on my door.

"Come in," I yelled for Onya to open my door.

"Momma, you want to watch *The Wrong Missy*?"

"Yeah, put it on in here. I need a good laugh. Let me shower first, I'll be right back." I told Onya rising from my bed.

After showering, I walked in my room laughing. Onya had our food, chips, and popcorn on a serving platter with bottles of water.

"Oh, it's a movie night," she yelled. We got comfortable on my bed and Onya started the movie. My phone chimed letting me know I had message. I opened the message **317-555-0989; He's mine now.** This nigga really gave a bitch my number.

"What is it momma?" Onya asked.

"Nothing." I responded.

I must talk to Damon about this, but I'll wait until he brings the boys back. I'm going to keep my peace by any means necessary. Even if it means killing a bitch. I don't care if he has a chick. She doesn't need to contact me on no childish shit.

Finally getting over the text message, Onya and I enjoyed the rest of the night. After the movie went off, we cleaned my bed off and Onya went to her room. I pulled out Monty number and dialed it.

"Monty" he said.

"Hi Monty, this is Kim. You g…"

"I know who you are." He stated cutting me off.

"Sorry to call so late but, I was wondering do you know a good divorce attorney?" I asked hoping he did.

"Never be sorry for anything," he said.

"Actually, I am a family attorney as well." He responded.

"I need your services," I said with hesitation.

"How about you come to my office on Monday, and we can discuss the process, no charge for the consultation."

"Ok, I see you Monday," I replied, speaking with joy.

"Never run from what you want. Go for it with full speed. Not just your divorce with everything you want out of life. I have seen many of hurt women. You want to be free from hurt, pain and disappointment. You don't have a revengeful spirit. You want to get a divorce and be done without the extra bullshit." He stated.

I agreed. "Monty, I appreciate your help, it's getting late, and lady must never be on the phone after ten." We laughed and said goodbye then disconnected the call.

Monday morning came I pulled in the front of The Law office of Monty Stapleton. I parked my truck and walked in the building.

"Good Morning!" A middle-aged woman said as I walked through the door of the one-story building.

"My name is Lisa," she said with smile.

"Good morning. I'm Kim Anderson," I said back.

"Kim, Monty will be with you shorty," she replied without hesitation.

"Thank you!" I responded taking a seat.

After a few moments, she spoke again. "Kim, Monty will see you now."

I followed Lisa through the hall to last office on the right.

"Would you like coffee, water or tea?" Lisa offered as she ushered me to have a seat with a smile on her face.

"No thank you." I said taking a seat.

Minutes later. Monty walked in the office wearing navy blue slacks, blue plaid button- down dress shirt, navy blue dress shoes and Burberry cologne.

"Good morning!" He said walking in with a smile as he extended his hand to shake mine.

Holding my right hand out, he placed both hands on my right hand and shook it once before letting go. He took a seat across from me.

"How is your morning so far?" He asked looking at me waiting for an answer.

"Not too bad, anxious to get this process started."

"What is it that you want from the divorce?"

"Full custody of my children, that's it. I have two children from a previous relationship."

"Do you want any monetary compensation?" He asked typing on his laptop.

"No," I responded shifting in my seat.

He looked up at me stunned by my answer. "How do you plan to care for your children financially? "He asked in a serious manner.

"Did I say something wrong?" I questioned.

"No," he replied shaking his head. "No matter what my client asks for I always get more," he smiled closing his laptop and walking to the printer.

He grabbed a sheet of paper off the printer and walked back over to me.

"Here is what it will cost to retain me."

My eyes popped out of my head looking at his figures.

"Thank you for your time, Monty." We shook hands and I walked out the office door.

Chapter Two

Damon

The night Kim shot me I was out celebrating Bump's opening of his second location of Rollin' and Growing Tire and Rim Shop. On my way home, I got a call from a nigga that owed me some money. We met up, I got my money, and went home asked Kim to put it away. Kim had one job. That was to put the money up, nothing else. She started talking about paying bills. The bills get paid. I felt like she was playing games. Games I don't play. She knew damn well I pay bills on time, not early.

I did take it too far by putting the shot gun to her head, but it was like something took over me. I looked at Kim in the face. She looked hurt, disappointed, and confused. I pulled her close to me while apologizing to her, but she was not having it. She pulled away with so much hurt in her eyes. I felt bad until she pulled the gun out. It shocked me that she shot me, of all people. I would never do anything to harm Kim. I never took Kim as a shooter. That reminds me to ask her about the gun.

Since Kim had left me, I found myself back with Keisha more often. To be truthful, I never l stopped messing with Keisha when Kim and I got married. We stopped having sex, but we would kick it here and there. She accepted everything about me, even my marriage. She had been staying the night at my house since Kim call herself moving out. She cooked, cleaned, and did everything without me having to ask her to do it.

She also did too much sometimes. She did sneaky stuff like going through Kim's closet. One day I left to check on the shop. When I came back, I eased in the house. Keisha was rummaging through Kim's things. After that, she could no longer be in my house alone. Lately some things have been off. Since becoming a realtor, she been traveling more. Good on her part, but if she thinks I am going to play the fool, she needs to bounce. If she is seeing someone one else, I couldn't care less. I'm leaving for a business trip in a couple of days so Keisha must bounce any way.

I really want my family home. Without them its' lonely and dead. Even with Keisha it's no life. I miss the boys making noise and me telling them to be quiet. I miss Kim and Onya cooking and laughing together. It's just not the same. Sometimes I stay out all night. I will fall asleep in my car in the driveway to avoid going in the house. So many times, I have I asked Kim to return home. She keeps shutting me down. What is it going to take to get my wife back?

The truth is I need to see a counselor, but I refuse to sit and tell someone my problems. My dad went MIA several years ago. He sends letters with no return address and that bothers the hell out me. I don't understand why he would leave us. I remember sleeping in my bed, "*Damon get up, put these clothes on," he said handing me a jogging suit with a t-shirt, socks and tennis shoes." "I'm sleepy daddy. I don't want to go." I cried. "SSSHH hush. Stand here," he said standing me in front of Denise's door while getting Denise out her baby bed. He picked Denise up and placed her in his arms and grabbed my hand as we walked to the car where he placed us in the backseat of his car closed the door and went back in the house. The car was facing the house. All I saw was flames. "Daddy, Momma," I yelled! I tried to get out the car, but he stopped me. "Momma" I yelled as he placed me back in the seatbelt. My cries woke Denise up and she started crying. "My dad got in the car and drove off. "Momma," I cried with tears pouring down my face. He looked at me through the rearview mirror but never said a word. Hours later we stopped for gas, food and he changed Denise's diaper. She was only a little over a year old.*

The entire ride from Atlanta to San Diego, all I could think about was my mother. We finally pulled up to a house where a brown skin lady with long black hair hung down to her mid back opened the door and stood on the porch while my dad retrieved Denise and I from the car.

"What took you so long sweetheart?" the lady asked before kissing his lips him.

"Not now," he responded. Inside, the house had classic black leather furniture, huge lion statues, black marble tables, and huge paintings of herself on each wall.

"Give me the girl, I'll lay her in my bed. Put him in the other room." She said taking Denise out my dads' arms. My dad followed the lady to her room with me holding his hand. Here lay him in here. My dad

laid me down on the bed and told me everything would be alright. He turned the lights off. Thinking of my mom I feel asleep.

The next day I woke to smell of food cooking. I got out the bed, "Daddy," I yelled but the woman came instead.

"Your daddy is out right now; he will be back shortly." She replied with a smile on her face.

"Will you call my momma?" I asked with sad face and tears running down my face? Her smiled instantly went away. My tears instantly stopped then I asked for Denise. The women smiled sneakily and took me in the kitchen with Denise sitting in a highchair playing in her grits. Just as she sat me in the chair at the kitchen table my dad walked through the back door. I got out the chair and took off running to him." Hey boy, what's wrong?" he asked looking confused."

"I want my momma; I want to go home." I responded hugging my dad.

"This is our home for a now. Your mom was feeling tired, so I sent her away. Momma will call when she feels better."

"Let's call to check on her, please," I begged but it did no good.

After, breakfast my dad bathed and dressed us for the day. We hopped in an all-black truck. Roxy drove for what seemed like hours. We parked in the parking lot. Roxy got out and we sat in the car. Roxy came back with bags in her hand. My dad got out to help her put the bags in the trunk.

"Dawson, why would you do that to Heaven? She was a sweet lady". Roxy asked. Hearing my momma's name, my three year old ears were

tuned in. What did he do to my mother I wondered? Where is my mother?

It seemed like every night I have the same dream rather nightmare and I want to know where my mother is. Here I am 36-year-old with no idea where my parents are. Why would my dad take us away from my mother and where is my father? Rather than dealing with my problems. I become so frustrated that I take it out on whoever is around when my mind goes on my parents.

Running the shop today was more tedious than any other day for some reason. I had to run errands most of day which had me missing Kim more. Kim was responsible for handling everything I was taking care of. She makes it look so easy. Now I realize I took her for granted. I never would have thought she would leave me. I called a local flower shop to have flowers delivered to the shop. I need my wife. Here it is going on two weeks and Kim refuse to come home. We are even now. I put a gun to her head, and she shot me. I say we move on. Fuck it! I'll give her some space. I hope she realize what type of man she has before it is too late. I not going to sit around long and wait for a woman to make her mind up.

In the meantime, I am on my way to San Diego to a business meeting and to visit my girls. Packing the last of my items I called Kim to make sure she would show up for work tomorrow, ordered red and white roses and put some money in her desk drawer. Although, she had moved out I felt obligated to make sure she was good. Besides since taking over she was doing a hell of job keeping up with the increase of demand. She fired a couple of my guys for putting their vehicles before the customers vehicles. Kim took business seriously and nothing was overlooked when it came to employee performance. I paid my employees top pay and I expected top service. Once they figured out who she was they treaded lightly.

Kim has me in a fucked-up mood. I must say. I'm trying to play it cool to get her back, but this is bothering me something serious. I have never missed anyone like this except my mother. This would be the perfect opportunity for us to get away for few days. But I need a reliable person to work the shop while I'm gone. Knowing, Kim she would not go anyway. I heard great things about Chains (Marquis Collins) in San Diego. He has his hands in dealerships, real estate, hair salons… too much shit to name. Hearing about Anderson Luxury Motorcycles, he hit me to ask if I was interested in opening shop on the West Coast. If there is a demand for bikes, I'm there. Our customer drove his customized bike to his dealership to purchase his wife a car and Chains wanted to meet the owner. Bump and I agreed to meet him tomorrow at his dealership to discuss the details.

It is 3:30 pm. My flight is out at 6:15 pm. I jumped in the shower and washed myself a couple of times. I grabbed a towel and dried off. Walking into my bedroom and sliding the closet door back, I grab a pair of black jeans and black sweater and put on my black Timberlands. Shit, I remembered I don't know the temp for the weekend.

Forget it! I grab a couple pairs of jeans and sweaters threw it in my duffle bag adding everything I might need. I called to let Bump know I was on my way out the door. I put my bags in my car and hopped in the car, backed my car out the driveway and headed towards the highway. Leaving the house 4:30 pm had me ahead of the evening traffic. Parking close to the shuttle pick up spot. I got my bag and locked my car up. Just as I approached the waiting area the shuttle pulled up. I got a spot sitting in the front of shuttle bus. Holding my things tightly I called Bump.

"I'm heading to check in I'm meet you in the boarding area."

"Cool" he responded and disconnected the call. Making my way through the busy crowd, I spotted an empty seat. "Damon!"

I turned around to be met by a smiling face.

"Hi Keisha" I said dryly.

"What are you doing here?" she questioned with a smile on her face. "

Why does it matter? Don't question me. He said in a firm voice.

"Boarding flight 305!" the stewardess announced over the intercom."

"That's us," Bump said as he walked by me side-eyeing Keisha while shaking his head.

Going through the final check point I made my way on the plane found my seat, pulled my phone out.

"Hell nah! Keisha get away from me! What would my Wife think?" I yelled before she could sit next to me.

Quickly changing her mind, she walked to back of plane.

"What is going through her mind?" Bump asked putting his phone on silent.

For the rest of the flight, I tried to relax my mind but this situation with Kim had me thrown. The plane landed. Bump and I headed to Hilton, got checked in, and went our separate ways.

"I'll hit you up in a minute." I dapped Bump up and headed towards the elevators, getting off on the 4th floor.

Walking off the elevator, I opened my room door. I threw my things down before I dropped down on the bed. I got my phone and dialed Kim.

"Hello!" Kim answered like I was bothering her.
"How did things go today?"

"Everything was fine. Have you made to your destination?" she inquired.

"Yes, I am laying down wishing you were here."

"Okay, well let me know when you get back."

"Kim stop playing with me," I said softly but boiling on the inside.

"Bye Damon," she said before the call disconnected.

Hearing my phone beginning to make noise I hurried to answer to answer it without realizing it was not Kim's ringtone.

"Stop playing with me!" I yelled.

"Damon, it's Keisha, what's your room number?

"Here you go questioning me again. I have something to take care of. I'll hit you later."

I needed something to take my mind off Kim and Keisha wasn't it right now. I called Bump to meet for a drink and to discuss tomorrow's meeting. After having drinks, I called it a night. I headed back to my room and noticed Keisha in the hallway. Ignoring her, I hurried to open the door and tried to close it, but she pushed it open, followed me in the room, and closed the door behind her. Instead of turning her away, I allowed her to stay in the room.

"You found me, huh?" I asked pouring a shot of patron.
I threw it back then poured another one.
"What a coincidence were staying in the same place. I can leave but you don't want me to do that." She stated in a seductive voice.

"I have a meeting tomorrow I need to prepare for, well at least get my outfit together."

She ignored me as she kicked off her heels and poured herself a shot of patron as well.

I walked into the bathroom, turned the shower on, undressed, and got in with her right behind me. Before I knew it, I had her bent over in the shower.

"Kim, I missed you!" I yelled.

"Damon! I know you didn't just call me Kim!" Keisha yelled. She quickly pulled away from me, got out of the shower, and put on whatever clothes she could as she headed for the door. She wasn't even fully dressed as she left the room cussing me out so loud all the other hotel guests had to be able to hear.

I went to get in the bed as if nothing happened. I told her ass years ago I loved my wife. She knew Kim and I are going through right now. My mind is on Kim. She wants to continue to play games as if it's just her and I. Although she did feel good, she wasn't as good as Kim. If Kim continues to be on this independent trip shit, I will keep Keisha around a little longer.

Looking at my phone, I noticed I had missed call from Kim. I was happy to at least get call, so I hurried to call her back. Since she has been gone the only conversations we have, are those I initiate.

"Hello" Kim answered.

"I was in the shower when you called."

"Just wanted to make sure you have everything you need for the meeting tomorrow."

"Yeah, everything except for you."

"I don't know who you gave my number to but tell her to stop texting my phone. I'll give you time to figure it out before I hurt her feelings. Let me know when you make it back in town," Kim said and disconnected the phone.

I called right back.

"Yes," she answered.

"STOP hanging the phone up before you make me upset. I am trying my best to deal with you moving out but don't hang the phone up on me again!" I yelled.

Kim sat on the phone quietly. Getting up to the go the restroom, I noticed Keisha left her underwear.

"Damn, she left her underwear." I said forgetting Kim was on the phone.

"Who left her underwear Damon?" Kim asked.

"What? I said I need to buy some underwear. Bye Kim." I knew Kim was not going for that. So, I disconnected the call and got in the bed for the night.

The next morning Bump and I met for breakfast then headed over to meet Chains. I got up to open the curtains. The sun was brightly shining. This is about to be wonderful day. I hopped in the shower thinking about this move. If everything comes together as I envision, this will be a wonderful partnership. After washing my body a couple of times, I grabbed a towel, dried off, wrapped the towel around my waist, and brushed pearly whites. I walked out the bathroom to a banging on the door. Looking through the peep hole I laughed at the person on the other side of the door. I opened the door and Keisha walked in with an attitude.

"I left my underwear here last night," she said looking around the room for underwear.

I closed the door and said nonchalantly "look in the trash can."

While I walked to the bedroom mirror to brush my goatee." Damon, we have been messing around since you have been married, not one time did you tell me you were coming to Cali. I gave you the common decency to inform you I was leaving. Yet, I see you at the airport." Keisha said walking towards me. "Keisha I am a married man. I am not obligated to tell you anything. If you got want you came for there's the door." I pointed in the opposite direction. Paying me no mind she snatched my towel down, took my wood, stroked it, placed in her mouth then went to work. I hollered out which made her go faster then she swallowed. Keisha got off her knees walked in the restroom. I grab a condom and put it on walked over to her in the restroom then bent her over the restroom sink then proceeded to bang her insides out. Hearing my phone ring with Kim's ringtone I pulled out immediately to answer the phone." Hey Kim! Is something wrong?" No, everything is good. I emailed you a list of things to go over before your meeting. Not important just things you would never think to discuss." She laughed. Making me laugh. "Damon!" Keisha yelled loud enough for Kim to hear her. "Bitch, I'm talking to my wife" I yelled out. "You have a female in your room?" Kim questioned. "No, it's the maid." I told Kim. "Bitch get out "I yelled at Keisha as I heard Kim taking a deep breath and call went dead. Keisha dressed in silence. "Why would you say anything when you see me on the phone? "Bitch learn how to play your position. I scold her as if she was my child. "Damon, if don't treat me better I will tell Kim about you and me. Now! You play your position." Keisha said boldly, turned to walk towards the door without looking back. Before she could reach the door handle. I jumped in front of her, causing her to freeze. Smiling in her face I told her "First thing first, don't ever say Kim's name without putting Mrs. in front of it." I laughed in her face then walked back to bedroom. Keisha slammed the door hard behind her. Putting on a pair of denim jeans and white shirt paired with white Nike placed my jewelry on, brushed my hair once again then headed to meet Bump.

Getting off the elevator same time as Bump.

"Mannnnn!! You would never guess what the fuck happened this morning."

Seating down in a booth, we picked up the menu simultaneously. The waitress came over to take our orders.

"May I have your drink orders" she asked.

"I'll have a water." I responded.

"I'll take a coke." Bump said looking up from his menu.

Telling Bump what happed over breakfast left him shaking his head.

"Damon on serious note you have to figure out if you want to stay married or not. Sooner or later your games are going to blow up in your face. I am telling you want I know."

"Thank you", Bump told the waitress as she placed our drinks in front of us and asked if we were ready to order.

"I'll take the steak, egg and potatoes." I responded looking at the waitress.

"I'll have the pancake platter." Bump gave his order before continuing his thought.

"Kim will either go crazy on you or leave you. He said with confidence.

"Amelia was nice and calm like Kim but after everything I took her through, she became a monster that I wish I would have left sleep. Man to Man. You should think about talking to a professional before you lose your wife for good. I've been knowing you since we were in grade school. No matter how big your pride is. I know when the home front is fucked up and right now it's fucked up" he looked at me and laughing.

"What the fuck is so funny?" I ask with my lip curled.

"Your ass is what's funny!" he said with a smirk on his face.

"Get this shit out your system. Not for Kim, for you" He said.

Everything he said was true but fuck it. Ride my wave or get the fuck gone. We talked until our food was brought out. Finishing our food, we paid the bill then made our way to meet Chains.

Pulling into the car lot I noticed an exquisite variety of vehicles parked closely together. We found a parking spot close to the front door. Parked the cars then hopped out. Bump and I looked at each other as we exited the cars.

"What could he possibly want to meet about?" I asked.

"He needs to invest in a larger lot." I said making Bump laugh.

By the looks of it he wasn't selling anything.

"Good morning, welcome to Collins Luxury Dealership!" A woman us greeted with a smile on her face.

"I have a meeting with Marquis! I'm Damon Anderson! This is Bump!" I stated.

"Mr. Anderson, right this way."

I Followed behind the petite woman. She walked us into his office.

"Damon! Glad you could make it!" Before I could introduce Bump, Keisha walked in.

What are you doing here? was going to be my question before Chains introduced Keisha as the realtor. I noticed the way they looked at each other. They were more than business partners. Deciding if I should keep it player or bust her ass out. I kept it player. I nodded my head at her. Chains continued with the meeting. When it was Keisha turn to give some background information. I chimed in.

"I thought you looked familiar. You grow up in the inner city of Indianapolis. We probably bumped into each or a time or two at other business meeting."

The look on her face was priceless.

"Yes, that's where I know you from. From doing busines with Mrs. Kim".

She said with a smile on her face. "Give her my regards."

She replied staring at me in silence. I was boiling on the inside. Wearing my poker face, I ignored Keisha. I agreed to expand Anderson Luxury Motorcycles but changing to name to Anderson's Custom Motorcycles. Chains took out shot glasses, filled it with Louis xiii then handed each of us one.

"To new business" he said with a raised glass.

Bump and I raised our glasses in "to new business." Keisha stood to side with smile on her face.

Leaving Chains office, we went our separate ways. Putting the entire fiasco with Keisha to back of my head. I put Alexandra's address in the GPS and headed to visit my daughters.

Looking at the address again. I must be paying too much child support. Before I could park the car. The girls came running out.

"Daddy," they yelled running into my arms.

Getting out the car I hugged all three of them. Noticing the girls attire I should not be surprised by the designer shit they wore. I knew Alexandra always had expensive taste. By any means necessary she would make shit shake. Walking up to Alexandra's house I noticed her landscaping was on point. The house was made of stone with a two- car garage.

"Hi Damon." She said dryly.

"Follow me" she said leading me to her sitting area.

The inside was just as immaculate at the outside. I sat down. She went to kitchen and brought out a bottle of water. She disappeared and Aubrey started talking about her dance classes.

"Alexander" I yelled!

"The girls and I are about to head out I'll bring them back later."

We hopped in the car. We pulled in Texas Roadhouse to eat.

"Daddy, can we go shopping", Audrey asked.

"Let's go."

 We headed to Fashion Valley mall where I pulled out three bundles each filled with two stacks a piece. Handing each on my girls two grand a piece making sure to inform them not to ask for nothing else until next month. They laughed at me like I was comedian. I was dead as serious. After walking through the mall with the girls. I took the girl's home. They had grown into little ladies. I would beat a nigga to death if they treated my girls how I treated Kim. I think it's time I got my shit together. Pulling back into Alexandra's home had me thinking it was time for an upgrade. Kim deserved a new home. She had been trying her best to make sure the home front was taking care of. Our house wasn't bad. It was time for an upgrade. It wasn't like I could afford it. I walked the girls in the house we said our goodbyes.

Backing out her driveway. Kim was calling.

"What's up pretty lady."

"How did the meeting go?" she asked with excitement.

"It was good. I'll be expanding out here. I'll name this one Anderson Custom Motorcycle's." I responded.

"Alright, talk to you later. I love you Kim."

I got in before she hung the phone up.

"Okay, Damon" she disconnected the call.

It was getting late. I headed back to the room. Getting off the elevator I noticed Keisha with Chains on her side. I contemplated if I should speak or leave them be. I decided to let them be. Once in my room. I poured me shot of patron took shower then called Kim. After several times of her phone going to voicemail. I sent a text. Kim: Why the fuck you didn't answer your phone? Becoming pissed I wanted to break her phone. I don't know who she thought she was playing with. I was dead as serious when I told her ain't no divorce. I would kill her before she be with another nigga.

A few minutes later Kim called back hollering at me.

"Damon, what is the matter with you? I was on the phone with you less than two hours ago. This behavior is totally unnecessary. Why do you continue to be aggressive with me? I feel like were enemies. Instead of husband and wife. If you continue go on like this, I will never come back to you. Matter of fact! Find someone to keep your attention."

I apologize Kim I want you with me. I miss you. That's all." I said trying to smooth things over.

Kim disconnected the call. I called her back and it went straight to voicemail. Fuck her. Thinking of Keisha. I called her. She answered on the first ring.

"Hello" she answered in a sexy voice.

"Bring your ass to my room." I told her.

"Hell no, you sound drunk. Plus, after you played me for Kim were done." She replied.

"Stop playing games. You know my wife comes first. The door is open."

I got out the bed to open the door. Keisha walked in wearing a black sheer shirt with black bra underneath, black yoga pants with black fur slippers. I love the sexy side of woman. Well in this case a hoe. She closed the door behind herself. I sat on the edge of the bed, pulled my boxers down. She slopped me down until I had enough. She thought she was going to slide on me.

"You can go now.

"I peeped how you brought my wife's name up. You and Chains are more than friends. That's between the both of you. Listen well. Don't mention my wife's name again in this little game you are playing." I said walking to restroom to relieve myself with a smirk on my face.

"Oh, now you are in you are feelings. Does your wife know I'm here in your room?" She asked in demeaning way.

"Chains and I are strictly business partners. He has a family" Keisha hollered back trying to convince me otherwise.

"Stop lying to yourself. The truth is you're a single lady so I can't tell you what to do. What we had is done. I don't care who you are sexting. It won't be me. Now get out." I said walking her to the door.

Before she could speak her peace. I closed the door as her foot passed the door frame. I wiped myself off, climbed in the bed and dozed off. Hearing my alarm go off at 4 am the next morning. I called Bump to make sure he was up to make the flight on time. I headed to the shower. Washing my body, a couple times I dried off. Dressing for Indianapolis weather I gather my things in my bag and headed downstairs. Meeting Bump in the lobby we drove the rentals back to the airport. We boarded the flight without running into Keisha. Relaxing in my seat I shot my realtor a text let him I know to find me a house fit for Kim.

Waiting for a response back, I must have fallen asleep. Hearing the stewardess on the intercom startled me waking me up from the dream concerning my parents. I got up from my seat to retrieve the overhead luggage. Grabbing our luggage Bump and I exited the plane. Walking out the airport. Amelia was there to meet Bump. But my ass had to walk to the shuttle spot.

Getting in my car I allowed it to warm up before I drove off. My phone began to ring. Seeing it was Paul I quickly answered it.

"What's up Paul? I hope you got some good news for me." I said without hesitation.

"I have house far north no H.O.A. Just liked you asked large and spacious. I know Kim will love it. Meet me at the house in an hour so you can look and tell me what you think.!" Paul said excited.

"Thanks Paul!" I said and disconnected the call.

Pulling up the address Paul sent over. I was amazed at what I was looking at vs the price. Getting out the truck and walking towards the side of the house.

"What do you think?

Where is Kim?" Paul asked looking inside my car.

"She had some personal things she was tending to." I said instantly becoming angry.

"I love it" answering the first question.

"Let's go inside" Paul said after we walked around the outside grounds.

 Realizing this a great deal I signed my name. Paul continued to go over details of the house.

"I have your money in the car."

"Mr. Anderson you fooled me." Paul said while play jabbing me!

"Your papers will finalize tomorrow." Paul said handing me a receipt and shaking hands.

"Kim and I will be by tomorrow around 1 pm!" I responded hopping in my car heading home to an empty house.

Before we move. I need to get Keisha totally out the picture. I called Keisha over so I could break it off with her. Instead, she ended up in my bed. She was shaking me telling me she cooked breakfast. Not sure how all this occurred but it had to end today. I about died when she told me I asked her to give me another chance. I was probably talking in my sleep. I know for a fact I was not talking to her. Our conversation became heated. She left and shattered my glass door. Cleaning glass up at 1 am was not fun. I found a 24- hour window replacement company open. Just so happen, they had a glass that fit my door perfect. Now that I was woke. I could not go back to sleep.

Chapter Three

Keisha

When Damon informed me he was getting married, I was devasted. He and Kim were everywhere together. They were at cookouts, weddings, open houses, any celebration they were there. Being that we hung with the same crowd, I was there too. Kim never paid attention to me. Had she not married Damon, I would not know her.

As time went on, it was Damon, no Kim. Hearing everyone ask about Kim had my blood boiling. It was always, she on vacation, she took the kids shopping. I wanted to snap his neck every time someone said Kim. Overhearing, he allowed her to run his business, I became enraged. I tried stalking Kim on Facebook, but I never found her. One day while hanging out with some mutual friends, Damon stopped by after coming back from taking Kim to Jamaica. Talking about how much fun they had without the kids. I had enough. I stormed out the door. Damon came running behind me.

What's going on with you?" he asked in a compassionate manner.

"I decided it was time for me to get myself together," I said looking at him while drinking a corona.

"You know I'm married. I'm not leaving my wife for you. What did you expect?" He waited for me to answer.

"I thought we could still be friends."

"We can, you are the one acting funny!" He lifted my chin, stared me in the eyes, and kissed me. Instead of pulling back, I allowed his tongue in my month. After that, we fooled around although he was distant. I was invisible while she was around. After a long talk we decided to keep it cordial.

Being interested in flipping houses, my cousin Naomi talked me into enrolling at Collins Real Estate School. Naomi took me in as her protégé'. With her helping me with the entire process, I went to six-figure income in less than seven months. That is how I met Marquis (Chains) Collins. While attending a conference in Indy, he was in attendance to support his up-and-coming relators. I was dressed to kill. I wore a red dress that stopped right below my knees. A nude pair of heels with my freshly done body wave bundles installed prevented him from being able to speak.

Lisa invited him to sit down with us. She introduced us. Noticing his wedding ring, I decided to listen to him and allow him to get his corny jokes out. Lisa excused herself leaving us alone at the table. As soon as we were alone, he asked me on a date. One date turned into him flying into town to see me. Next thing I know, he was flying me out to visit him. Before I knew what was happening, we were in a relationship. He was everything I needed in a man. He was attentive, smart, and wealthy. The only problem was, he was married.

I knew to run and not look back, but I was so drawn into him. It wasn't that I needed his money. He was treating me how I desired to be treated. His wife was never a problem unlike Kim. He didn't flaunt her around, but her presence was known. Chains was dedicated to his children. Other than that, he did whatever his wife asked to keep her happy. Although he reneged on a couple dates that wasn't the normal for us. He would make time for me.

"Lisa I'm about to head to the airport." I yelled out to my older sister, whom I shared a three-bedroom condo with while my house is being built.

"Here I come," Lisa yelled running down the stairs.

We grabbed each other and rocked side to side. "Keisha, I am so proud of you. Make sure you lock the deal down and bring home coins," Lisa said with a smile on her face.

Lisa had no idea that I was meeting Chains in San Diego. He had a potential new business partner he was bringing out to hopeful open a new business. Lisa had been on me for months to leave Chains alone. If she knew I was in and out of Damon's bed too she would throw a fit.

When Chains told me he was married, I didn't flinch. I'd already seen his ring, so I knew what I was doing from the jump. So, in response to his confession, I simply smiled and said, "I know how to play my position, but it will cost you."

He tongued me down something serious and handed over his bank card. Besides, how does she think my house is being built? Lisa is what I call a goody to shoes. If it is not, morally right she wants no parts of it. Me, I enjoy living on the wild side. Besides, Chains lives in Cali. Luckily, my stock went up. I don't have play with small timers. Damon's stingy ass is about to be the thing of the past.

My phone beeped indicating my uber was waiting. Walking outside the morning breeze was stronger than I anticipated. I was dressed for San Diego's weather not Indianapolis. The driver got out and put my luggage in the trunk. On the way to the airport while scrolling on my Facebook, an old memory of Damon and I popped up. I thought I deleted all his pictures, but I decided not to let the memory mess with my head. Damon was yesterday. Chains is tomorrow.

When I arrived at the airport, the Uber driver opened my door and took my bags out of the trunk. I was pleased with his service, so I reached into my purse and handed him a cash tip instead of adding it on the app. I walked inside, checked in, and checked my luggage.

Walking through the airport, I looked down at my watch I had about forty-minutes to spare. Entering the boarding area, I found an empty seat facing the crowd. To my surprise and disappointment, my eyes landed on Damon.

"Damon," I yelled out. "What are you doing here?" I asked smiling.

Damon did not reply. I was in his bed less than twenty-four hours ago. He did not mention anything about taking a trip. I told him I had business out of town for a couple days. He said okay, that was it. Now here he is refusing to answer my question. Before I could show out, it was time to board the flight. I got ready to sit between Damon and Bump and Damon shot me down quickly. Instead arguing I made my way to the back of plane, then called Chains to let him know I was on the plane. Getting comfortable in my seat I started dreaming of fish. I woke up to hearing the landing announcement.

Once I was off the plane, I looked around for Damon and he was nowhere in sight. I called Chains to let him I was headed out. He was outside waiting for me. He walked to me with open arms as his light skin glowed brightly as Cali's sun hit it. We embraced briefly and released each other. He grabbed my luggage then placed them his 2020 Tahoe. He held my hand as I climbed in SUV. Closing my door, he walked around, entered the driver side and we took off.

We held hands while he drove to the hotel. Pulling up to Hilton making small talk, I noticed Bump and Damon walking in through the entrance. Parking the truck, he got out, walked around to open my door. We walked up to concierge desk to check in. Chains handed me the key card. He placed his hand in the small of my back as we headed to the elevator. Getting on the elevator, Chains' phone rung.

I rolled my eyes. I already know where this was going. The door couldn't open soon enough. I quickly headed to my room while Chains straggled along talking on his phone. Walking in the room, he placed my luggage in front of the closet, finished his conversation, then the disconnected the call.

"Go ahead and leave, no explanation needed," I stated with a curled lip.

"Before I go, we need to pick you up a rental car."

I bent over to pick my purse up that I tossed in the chair, but it landed on the floor. He walked up to me. "Aht AHT!" I said waving my finger no. "Not if you are going home to the wife."

He didn't like when I told him no, but he didn't argue with me. Instead, he got himself together, picked the car up, and went home to his wife.

When I got back to the room, I grabbed my phone to facetime Lisa.

"Hey sis!" Lisa sang.

"Hey! I'm staying at the Hilton."

"Glad you made it safe. I'll call you back later I have a client walking in love you!"

"Love you too!" then her face disappeared.

Being that it was early afternoon, I decided to take nap. Waking up from my nap two hours later, I decided to dress and find out what San Diego had to offer. I put on a white tank top, and an adidas floral sweat suit with a pair of white vapor max, silver Donna Karen hoops with my long black bundles hanging down my back. I grabbed my Gucci floral backpack and headed out the door. Coming through the lobby, I noticed Bump walking with a guy I have never met before.

"What's up Bump?" I asked hoping he would introduce me to his friend.

The guy and I made eye contact.

"What's up Keisha?" Bump said and continued walking never introducing me to his friend.

Making my way downstairs and having my car brought around, I hopped in. While driving around, I found a Zaxby's, ordered food to go, then headed out. Instead of going back to the room, I drove around a little bit while I ate my food. When I walked back into the hotel lobby, I heard live music. Listening intently, I followed the noise. I found a seat in back out of the way. I looked up from the drink menu and my eyes laid on the dark chocolate guy with Bump earlier. This time Damon was with them having drinks and laughing, having a good time. I ordered a drink and finished it just in time to follow Damon back to his room. He was so intoxicated. He walked in his room and tried to close the door, but I pushed it open enough for me to squeeze in then closed it behind me.

Knowing he would accept my advances, I pushed the restroom door opened and followed him to the shower. Figured why not shower with him. I undressed and hopped

58

right in there. I bent over giving him a full access to enter through the backdoor. Just as it was starting to get good, he slipped up and called me Kim. This nigga calling me Kim was disrespectful. I hurried out the bathroom leaving my underwear on purpose hoping Kim would find them. With our history, I knew I would be his wife soon. It did not matter if we both were in relationships with other people. We would always get back together.

Seeing Damon in Chains office the next day had me shaking on the inside. I played it off as best I could. When Chains asked me to come to Cali, I saw dollar signs disregarding any other details. Now I was regretting that decision, but I needed to keep it together until after the deal closed and I got my cut.

After Damon and Bump left the meeting, I questioned Chains about their relationship. He pulled me into him wrapping his arms around my waist kissing my neck between his words.

"We met through a mutual customer." He stated.

I had no idea I would end up in the room with two men I was secretly seeing. Damon and I grew up in the same neighborhood on the far eastside of Indianapolis. We had history, but my relationship with Chains was new and promising. I couldn't let what I had with Damon mess that up. Well, at least until I could get Damon away from Kim. Then Chains could go back to his wife. His phone interrupted our make out session.

"Hey baby," he answered smiling making me roll my eyes while removing his hands from around me.

"The meeting went well. I'll see you at home tonight. Put on something sexy for me."

He said then ended the call. Walking back over to me with a serious look on his face, he backed me up against the wall. My heart was pounding. He unzipped my pencil skirt while kissing me. My arms wrapped around his neck.

He picked up me up and banged the inside of me saying, "If you can't handle me being married you can walk away."

I moaned in understanding. After we both released a couple times, he washed me then he headed home to be with his wife. I knew Damon would bring up Chains in the conversation, but he never did. Once again, he played me as if I am violin. When he put me out his room, I ran into dark chocolate as I call him. I was walking down the hallway furious when he started a conversation with me.

"What's up with you, you alright?" he asked.

"Yeah, I just need to get to my room," I said holding my head down.

He was exactly what I needed, something to ride on. Opening my door, we make it to bed and before I knew it, one leg was over his shoulder calling him chocolate. We went round for round running out of condoms.

"Now what?" he asked.

Before I could respond he was bare backing me. I couldn't tell him no. Falling asleep after a night of loving making, I woke to an empty bed. Getting out the bed, I almost fell from having noodle legs. Making it the shower I turned the water on thinking about dark chocolate. Dressing for weather back at home, I throw on some red jeans, red sweater, a pair of red booties. Looking in the mirror, I was ready to go home.

Who would have known rekindling a fling with Damon would have me in his house cooking breakfast a little after midnight. Before I break it off with Chains, I needed to make sure Damon is fully committed to me. Men speak sweet nothings while having sex.

"Damon," I yelled pushing him back and forth.

"Wake up I cooked fried potatoes, bacon, pancakes, biscuits."

I handed him the tray and placed a glass of orange juice in front of him. Sitting up we exchanged a kiss. I got back in the bed and sat next to him while he ate.

"Last night you said you wanted to give me another chance. Is that true?" I asked rubbing his back.

He started choking. "I SAID WHAT?" He hollered.

"You heard me," I said in a defensive voice.

"I'm married to KIM," he said after taking a drink of his juice.

"Then why the fuck am I here?" I yelled getting of the bed.

"Because you want to be here," he responded while he shrugged not caring how he made me feel.

"Somethings never change with you. I'm going to shower," I said walking towards the bathroom.

"No, you are not, go ahead and leave I have business I need to take care of." He bluntly said.

I don't understand why I wasted my time with him. I turned my nose up and finished putting my shirt on.

"You just fucked up. I am not a woman you can toss back and forth believe that."

I grabbed my jacket swinging my hair as I walked out his front door. Slamming it so hard I heard shattered glass as the door closed.

Chapter Four

Kim
November

It was the middle of Autumn. Leaving work at 7 pm, I decided to stop by Louise's house instead of going home. It was Thanksgiving Eve. My dad took the children out of town for the weekend. I hopped out my truck and rang her doorbell.

Opening the door Louise yelled, "What up gurly?" walking towards the sofa with me behind her.

"Nothing, I stopped by before going home. Umm. It smells good in here," I said as I took off my boots and placed them by the door.

I sat down and Peaches, Louise's daughter came in the living from the kitchen.

"Cousin!" she yelled."

"Hey Peaches!" I said getting up giving her a hug.

"What brings you by?" Louise asked.

"Did you forget I told you I was coming by after work, where is Damon?" She questioned with a raised eyebrow.

"We've been separated for about a month ago now," I shot back looking at her sideways. "I haven't talk to you in while, well not about that!"

"I knew something was going on with you. You kept talking about I'm okay." Louise used an imitation of a baby's voice.

"He put a shot gun to my head, and I shot him in the arm," I said taking a drink of water Peaches had placed in front of me.

Silence took over.

Louise finally said, "I told you before you married him to leave Damon alone. Now here you are possibly facing jail time for a situation that could have been avoided she yelled."

"That was months ago. He won't tell the police anything. I am surprised he has not tried to kill me," I told Louise nonchalantly.

"Girl you are crazy!" Peaches said laughing making drinks.

"He has been trying to get me to come home. I'm not ready yet. He hurt me really bad this time."

"What is your plan?" Louise asked while filling her glass up with wine.

"I've been staying at the old house. I'm working at the shop," I responded taking a deep breathe.

Louise and I sat and laughed while catching up for a couple more hours before I decided it was time to go. "I'm about to head out," I said getting up from the sofa. "I'll talk to you another day."

We said our goodbyes. I got in the truck and drove in silence.

The next morning hearing my doorbell startled me. I instantly I sat up. Looking at the clock next to my bed 4:46 am. I snatched the covers off me, grab my robe hollering who is it with my gun in my hand as I walked to the front door. I looked through the peephole and instantly my blood started to boil.

"Damon what is it? Do you know what time it is?" I asked opening the door.

Without answering my question, he made his way to living room. "Get your purse and come on your coming home."

Instead of arguing, I threw on jogging pants, a sweater, and boots. I grabbed my purse, locked the house, and hopped in his BMW with him closing the door behind me.

"See that's better," he said backing out the driveway driving to the northside.

"We can go to sleep in each other arms like old times," he said as I dozed off. The car slowing down woke me up. "Damon, I really don't want to be here."

"Stay with me until later. I just want to sit, talk, and cuddle."

Giving in, we went inside the house. Looking around everything seemed the same. As I sat down on the sofa something didn't feel right. "Somebody's been in my house" I yelled.

"Nobody's been here but kids," Damon said.

"No, it's a different spirit in here," I retorted.

"Are you seeing someone? If so that's cool. I have already contacted a divorce lawyer, but I hoped we could figure it out ourselves with getting attorneys involved," I said easing into getting a divorce.

"I am not seeing anyone," Damon tried to convince me, but I know better.

Whoever she was Damon had better be prepared for the fallout behind whatever situation he's trying to conceal.

Being that it was 5:30 am, I went to the guest room for a nap with Damon right behind me trying to convince me to go to our bedroom.

"Nope. This room is fine," I said laughing, pulling the covers back and climbing under the covers.

"Take your clothes off. You know you going to start sweating. I'm just going to lay here and hold you," he said laughing showing his white teeth.

Watching him smile brought joy to me. We laid down realizing it was Thanksgiving.

"Happy Thanksgiving," I told him.

He said it back then fell asleep. Damon tossed and turned for a few minutes then he stopped. Drifting back off to sleep, I woke to the doorbell ringing around twelve noon. I went to answer it, but no one was there. Thinking nothing of it I closed the door.

"Who was at the door?" Damon asked.

"Nobody."

He pulled his camera up trying to be discreet. Whoever it was hit a nerve. His face wrinkled up.

"What is it? I asked, knowing he was pissed.

"Nobody like you said," he said.

Instead of arguing I let it go. Damon went to the kitchen and started seasoning steaks and shrimp. He sauteed the onions and green peppers in the pan then added the steak.

"Kim, I know I fucked up. I have apologized several times. Yet, you never apologized for shooting me in the arm," he whined.

"I am not sorry that's why I have not apologized. Next time you pull a gun on me, you better kill me or I'll kill you," I said looking directly in his eyes.

He attempted to scare me by making a quick move. I stood right there unfazed thinking his demons are really trying me today.

"Now what? I am ready to go," I said in a harsh voice.

"You are really trying my patience. Calm the fuck down. I will take you home as soon as we eat," he said while removing the steak from the skillet.

My phone dinged let me know I had a text message.

"Who is that?" Damon asked.

"Probably a text notification," I said taking glasses from the shelve filling them with ice.

"Check it might be important."

"317-555-9878: He's mine Now!"

"You are exactly right. It is important," I told him showing him the text message. "It's the invisible ghost again," I said rolling my eyes.

He had a surprise look on his face.

"Do you know who this is?

"No, I don't recognize the number," Damon said, lying through his teeth.

The way his eyes widened let me know he knew who it was.

"This is the second time I have received this same message. If you are seeing someone, you need to let me know. I don't take bitches playing on my phone lightly. I am telling you now, I will blow someone's head off, including yours," I said taking a seat at the dining room table meaning exactly what I said. I was so upset; I lost my appetite.

If I would have had some grits, I would have thrown them on his face to remove his smirk. Trying to control my temper, I rose from the table walking to the back of the house telling Damon to take me home.

Damon walked behind me saying, "If I were seeing someone, I would tell you."

"You wouldn't tell me unless you want a divorce. Tell me then Damon." I stopped to face him. "Tell me you have a friend or someone because for me to get a message like this!" Holding up my phone. "Has your name written all over it. Remember this is the same bullshit you were doing before we married. This time I moved out and here you again pulling me back in your bullshit. Handle your business Damon and leave me out of it."

Damon left the house. I threw my hands in the air and hollered. I was tired of Damon's shenanigans. I started my bath water. I went to my closet and could instantly tell someone had been rummaging through my clothes. I found a Fendi dress I bought a few months ago still in the hanging bag. I pulled it out laid it across the bed. Looking in my drawer, I pulled out some personal items and placed them on bed alone with some jewelry. Walking to the restroom, I heard the doorbell ring. Looking on the camera I could tell it was a woman. I walked to the door to open it.

"May I help you?" I asked the brown skin lady.

"No, I have the wrong house," she said and walked away getting in an Audi and driving away.

I closed the door and walked back to the restroom. Something was not sitting right in my spirit about this woman. I felt an uneasy feeling sweep over me. I shook it off and said a prayer of protection. The dream I had months ago of me in jail cell played in my head. If I ever go to jail, I will have a valid reason, but a man is not one. Washing up and getting out, I heard Damon come in the house with bags in his hand. I heard the bags rubbing together as he passed the door. I grabbed my towel wrapped around me. He looked at me like I was meal.

"Nope, don't think about it," I said getting dressed.

"Where did that dress come from? You didn't have any bags when I picked you up," Damon questioned.

"That was only thing in the closet that the invisible ghost didn't touch," I said curling my hair.

Looking on the bed, I opened the bag and pulled out a pair of jeggings and sweater to match with the personal items.

"Leave that dress on. It's perfect for the occasion."

"What occasion?" I questioned putting on my black boots.

"I have something I want you to see," Damon said while changing his clothes.

Shortly after, we headed to the car. A car drove by the house. His entire demeanor changed. Looking down the street it looked like the Audi that was here recently.

"Are you okay?" I asked in concerned manner.

"Yeah, I'm good" He answered starting the engine than backed out the driveway.

Turning into traffic, where are we going?" I questioned.

"Just relax I got you." He suggested rubbing my legs.

"While you were shopping a woman came by in an Audi but, said she had the wrong address.

"I don't know who she is. She had the wrong address."

Damon tried it.

"But, nah, I don't believe she had wrong house. She was surprised I answered the door. This is getting to become an issue for me. I told you to move on but for you to lie about its unnecessary drama that going to cause a lot of problems. You can tell the truth about it or like anything else the truth will come out."

"Kim! I would tell you if I was seeing someone. Who are you to lie to?" He said trying to make a point.

"Your wife. The wife you want back in the home with you. The wife you cater to. Do I need to continue?" I asked in sarcastic manner.

Damon drove in silence turning the radio up. Thirty minutes later we made to our destination. My eyes grew wide looking at the site before me. We drove in straight then into a circular driveway. He stopped at the front door entrance. Looking out the passenger window had me in a trance.

"Whose house is this?" I questioned?

"This is our house if you want it.

"Every time, I walked in the other house it reminded me of the things that transpired. When I walk into the bedroom all I see is the chaos from that night. I called our realtor and this what he had available. I apologize for everything I have done. Accept this as my apology."

Looking at Damon I allowed everything to go in one ear and out the other. How many times does one apologize? How many times do I have to forgive? I asked myself before Seventy times- times seven came to mind.

"Kim did you hear me?" He asked becoming frustrated.

"Yes, I heard you. I accept the house as a good gesture. Forgiveness will come in time." I responded opening the car door in awe looking at the house.

Damon jumped out the car pulling out the key rushing to open the door.

"This is what I call a baby mansion."

"Speak up!" Damon said walking by my side.

"I was talking to myself," I responded walking to front door.

When he opened the door my, mouth hit the floor. I walked in the house and stood there for a moment. The three-story brick house was beautifully built. I took a slow walk through the house. Custom molding, high ceilings, five bedrooms, three car garage, home theater, home office, and best of all oversized master suite, with built in fireplace! I became excited thinking how I was going to decorate the house.

"Welcome home!" Damon said walking towards me as I was looking out the living room window into the huge yards.

I turned around and stared at him for a minute before walking into the master suite. Making my way through the room I noticed a tub with jets.

"Damon, I need cleaning supplies so I can enjoy this tub right now," I yelled out while walking out the room.

"Come here I have something I want you to see." Damon said walking out the door.

I walked around to other side of the room. Noticing, I was behind him, he opened the French doors to the walk-in closet and I jumped up down like I had won the lottery. This was another room. Hearing the lyrics *my rooms got rooms.* My closet was filled clothes from the old house that had tags still on them, alone with new clothes, shoes, purses, and jewelry. Not everything was designer or named brand, it's the thought that counts. I walked to him hugging him.

"Thank you, Damon."

He looked at me and smiled. Turning him a loose I went through the rest of the house.

Needing things for the house, we headed to Walmart for some basic items. Walking hand in hand we browsed the store talking and laughing like we had a perfect relationship. I decided to pay for the items since he purchased the house. The look on his face priceless when I pulled out my card. Laughing, I moved out of the way so he could put the bags in the cart. Damon pushed the cart to the car. He opened the door for me to get inside the car while he put things in the car. Reaching to open his door, he hopped in rubbing his hands together to warm them up.

"I really do want our marriage to work. Find me a counselor. I have some many unanswered questions from my childhood."

Damon disclosed his memories of his parents. My mouth dropped opened. Oh, my goodness. Listening to him pour his heart out to me, tears ran down my face. I rubbed his leg as he drove. We returned to the house and Damon parked the car in the driveway. We removed the bags in silence. Once inside the house, I put the things away then cleaned the tub. I ran him some bath water. I poured him a glass of Hennessy to relax him a little bit. What he shared was heartbreaking. Just thinking about what he said my heart went out to him.

Moving around in my kitchen felt good. I started to batter my pork chops while the grease got hot. Hearing my phone ring. I answered.

"Hello!"

"Bring your fine ass up here up here," Damon said.

"I just turned the stove on so the grease will burn if I come up there," I stated with my hands on my hips.

"Turn that shit off. We can order some food and have it delivered. I want you next to me." He said in a non-threating manner.

Putting everything away and cleaning the kitchen, I made my way up the spiral staircase. Entering the bathroom, Damon had scented candles lit and a glass of Hennessy waiting for me. After bathing, he turned the fireplace on. We got into bed, and I allowed him to fall asleep in my arms. Ending the night on a good note is what we needed.

The next morning Damon woke up before me. The smell of food entered my nostrils. Looking at my phone, it was 7:45 am. Damon had steaks, eggs, grits, biscuits, and apple butter on a marble plate next to a large glass of orange juice. He leaned to kiss my lips.

"How are you this morning? Last night was rough."

"I feel lighter since getting it out."

Sitting next to me Damon began to go over todays plans. He looked at me.

"Kim!" he yelled.

"What?" I hollered.

"Did you hear me?" He asked.

"No, this food is delicious! Did you cook this?" I asked him before stuffing my mouth.

He shook his head and walked away. I laughed and took a drink of my juice. Shortly thereafter, Damon entered the room again.

"We need to go by Paul's office to pick up the deed and start packing the other houses up for the movers."

Getting out the bed, I went to shower while Damon took my dishes downstairs. Feeling refreshed, I put on a pair of Nike leggings with the matching sweater and a pair of black furry boots.

"Are you sure you're going to pack?" Damon commenting kissing me on my cheek laughing.

"Let me grab my coat. I'll meet you downstairs." I said putting on my lip gloss.

Making my way downstairs I heard Damon on the phone laughing hysterically.

"What's so funny?" I asked smiling.

"Something came up at the shop. I'll take care of it later."

On the drive to my house Damon phone was ringing more than normal. Becoming curious I asked, "Damon is it something I need to know?"

"No, Kim. I got it. Just pack your house up. I called momma, she is going to keep the children with her until tomorrow, then they can come home and put their room together," he said sounding irritated.

We pulled into the driveway. He opened the door for me and walked me in the house. We engaged in a passionate kiss then he left. It took me a couple hours to pack all I was going to pack. I put some of the children's clothes in my truck and headed back home.

Chapter Five

Damon

Just walking Kim in the house, I missed ten missed calls. I made an appointment to meet the movers at nine. Running behind schedule, I had twenty minutes to make it to the other side of town. I just hopped on 465 to make it in record time. My plan was to have Kim's truck and the furniture delivered before she decided to start her day, but since I overslept, I took Kim to her truck so I wouldn't hear her mouth.

Hearing my phone ring, I answered it through the Bluetooth system.

"Hello!"

"I guess Kim came back," Keisha said with an attitude.

"Don't come back to my house without being invited," I said ending the call.

"Yes?" I answered as she called right back.

"I am done with you. I was your shoulder to cry on, now you think you can push me to side like a used doll. This is the last time you put Kim before me. I'm not going to continue to play your games. You could have told me she came back. I can be with somebody else. Goodbye!" Keisha finished her thought then disconnected the call.

I am glad she dismissed herself. Looking at my phone six of the missed calls were from Keisha. Pulling up to the front of house, I noticed the movers were backed in waiting on me. Going into the house I got chills. Not wanting to bring old memories to the new house. I hurried to make a couple of phones calls and furniture was sold just like that. About three hours later the house was empty and only the children's belongings were going the new house. Backing out the driveway. I did a double take. I know that's not Keisha riding past my house. I dialed her number.

"Yes, sweety" she answered in a sexy voice.

"Keisha, where are you? I need to talk to you." I told her.

"I'll be there in few minutes." She confirmed.

Before I disconnected the call all the way, she pulled in front of me and exited the car walking towards me. I waited until she got closer to my car. I got out my car with my face frowned. She attempted to run.

"Come here!" I yelled before she could get back in her car.

I grabbed her by neck. "Don't come by my house no more. I just told your ass that. Damn, do you listen?" I yelled.

She was hitting me and trying to get away. "Damon I am pregnant."

I dropped her instantly. She sat on the ground breathing hard trying to regain her strength. I helped her to her feet. "You and I both know that baby is not mine. You should try Chains, don't try me," I said with gritted teeth.

Rising from the ground she held her neck while walking to her car. Holding the door open she yelled, "How would Kim feel about being a step- mom?" She then slammed the door and drove off.

By the time I got finished picking up Kim's belongings and having the furniture delivered the house it was three in the afternoon. I pulled up to the house with Bump and Amelia in tow.

"Damon this is a nice house. I know Kim is loving this!" Amelia said with a smile on her face walking up to the house.

Unlocking the door, I noticed Kim had arranged some of the items that were delivered. Kim placed a family portrait of her and the children on the wall in formal dining room. I wonder how much she spent on that furniture that shit is heavy.

"Kim, Kim!" I yelled but she never responded.

"Go ahead and have a seat let me get Kim." I said while going in search for Kim.

"What are you doing woman?" I asked as I walked through the bedroom seeing her in the restroom smiling.

"What does it look like? I am taking a bath. Matter of fact hand me a towel and help me out." She said letting the water out the tub.

Grabbing a towel, I helped Kim out the tub. We walked in the room. Kim dried herself off, sprayed on her Burberry perfume and started putting on a black wide leg jumpsuit with some black clogs.

"Bump and Amelia are downstairs!"

"Good! "She said walking into her closet with a full-size vanity station fixing her hair.

"Where are you going?" I asked Kim while noticing how good and tasty she looks.

"Amelia and I are going to the nail salon." "Did you have something planned for us?" She questioned with a raised eyebrow.

"Let's go to dinner nothing fancy."

"Okay, after I get my nails done." She stated with a smile on her face.

"That's cool!" I said rubbing my hands together.
Kim finished getting ready, made her way downstairs greeting Bump and hugging Amelia. Oh, Kim you look good! Kim twirled around saying thank you and complimented Amelia on her long flowy maxi dress. I hated when Kim wore clothes to hug her body, but this outfit had me turned on.

"Let's go," I said ending their reunion.

"You cool Damon?" Bump asked.

I wanted to take Kim upstairs and take a nap, but I couldn't tell Bump that. "Yeah, lets ride out."

Amelia and Kim hugged us saying their goodbyes. I opened door following Bump and Amelia out.

Bump hopped in the car with me and Kim rode with Amelia in her Bentley coupe. "What's good Damon?" Bump asked.

"I got a call from the new manager at the pizza shop saying Keisha been up there showing out making me lose business, so they put her out. Then she called questioning me about Kim. I thought that was the end of it. Leaving the old house this morning, Keisha rides by, I had to do a double take."

"What is she on?" Bump asked in confusion.

"I told you to leave her alone when you first started messing with her. That girl is crazy. She is upset that you are back with Kim," Bump said.

"Yep, now she claims to be caring my child. If Kim's finds out about this. I am not sure what's going to happen." I stated looking at my phone.

"Look Bump. Keisha calling again."

"What Keisha?" I answered.

"What time should I expect you at my house?" she asked seductively.

"I'm not coming to your house."

"Yes, you are. Do you want your wife to find out about our baby?"

Taking a deep a breath I disconnected the call.

"Do you plan to continue to see Keisha?"

"I don't have choice."

"I would tell my wife and bite the bullet. She wouldn't continue to threaten me like that unless you don't care about your wife," Bump said sympathetically.

The ride over to Bump's was long and quiet except Pokey Bear's *My Sidepiece* was playing in the background. At this point, my peace was being taking away by my piece. Pulling up to Bump's gate he opened it with his fob, and we entered. I had never paid attention, but his shit was nice.

We walked in and immediately poured a couple drinks to get our mind right. Following behind Bump, we entered his man cave. Bump walked behind the bar and handed me a shot D'usse XO. I tossed it back and he gave me two more shots. "Alright Bump thanks for the shots. I'm about to head out."

"Alright Damon be careful."

We man hugged and I hopped in my car and headed to see Keisha. On the ride over, I was thinking if I really wanted to play Keisha's game. Keisha lived on the wild side which I didn't mind until today. I planned to get to the bottom of it. My phone starting ringing. Shit. Kim was calling.

"Hello," I answered not wanting to lie to Kim.

"Hey, Damon I'm done with my nails. Where do you want me to meet you?"

"That was quick," I responded giving me time to think of something.

"I just needed a fill-in," she responded.

"Go home and I'll meet you there," I told her to keep from lying to her.

"I'm tired. Once I go in and get settled, I'm not coming back out. I'll pick me up something and get yourself something before you come in."

"Okay," I said, and we disconnected the call.

Kim always did that. When she gets in her feelings she won't cook. Pulling into Keisha driveway, I was mad as hell. She has a house full of guests.

"Keisha, I yelled" walking in looking around.

All eyes were on me.

What's up babe?

"What is this?" I asked ready to walk back out the door.

"I invited some friends over so we could enjoy my friends as well."

I looked at her and walked right out the door.

"Damon, Damon!" Keisha called out behind me.

"What!" I turned to look at her.

"You don't mind if I tell wifey about us," holding her phone up while walking closer to me showing me pictures of us together with a smile on her face while rubbing her stomach.

"Don't contact my wife anymore. What is wrong with you? You have a man. Leave my wife alone. If I hear you contacting her again you will regret it." I told her, hopped in my car, and left.

Calling Kim back she didn't answer. I called back and she answered on the first ring.

"Hello, what did you get to eat?"

I decided to cook a pot of spaghetti, fried catfish nuggets with a salad."

"Okay, I'll be there shortly," I said before I disconnected the call. Twenty-five minutes later, I pulled in the driveway and parked by Kim's truck. Got out ready to eat and call it night. I did just that.

Chapter Six

Kim

Amelia and I rushed to her to 2019 Bentley Coupe knowing we were pushing the limit to making it the nail salon on time. I got in on the passenger side and put my seatbelt on. Swerving in and out of traffic Amelia was handling her car. I was starting to feel like I was riding on a rollercoaster. Amelia looked at me and burst out laughing.

"Loosen up!" She said turning the radio up.

"How is school coming along?" I asked Amelia.

"Let me say Bump got me this as an incentive to finish!" Amelia expressed dancing in her seat smiling!

"I can wait to see your graduation gift!" We both laughed as she pulled in the parking lot and parked.

"Good evening, ladies!" Lisa said as we walked in.

Amelia walked to Lisa's chair while I took a seat.

"Hey Lisa, this is Kim!"

"Hi," I said. Before I could get my butt in the chair.

Lisa was telling me to have a seat next to Amelia. Walking to my seat, Lisa gave me some crazy vibes.

"Kim, you look familiar! Do we know each other?"

Not thinking too hard, "No, I don't think so."

A nail tech came over and begin working on my nails.

"Kim, do you want to grab some food after this?" Amelia asked.

"I can't. Damon asked if I wanted to grab something to eat this evening!"

"Oh, you're Damon's wife!" Lisa said like she figured out the mystery causing Amelia and I to look at each other, then her.

"Yes, how do you know Damon?" I asked.

"We have mutual friends."

"Humm, interesting! I could see that. He's extremely popular," I said knowing she was lying.

"Lisa, I've been knowing you for years and I didn't know you knew Damon. He and my husband are best friends. Who are your mutual friends?"

Amelia asked waiting for Lisa to respond. It took her a minute to answer the questions.

"I dated a guy that knows Damon and he introduced us, that's it!"

Taking a deep breath, Lisa continued. "I don't owe you an explanation, but I respect our friendship."

"And being married to a Boss the disrespect can get real!" Amelia pointed out never taking her eyes off Lisa.

"Amelia, it's cool! What's done in the dark all always comes to light," I intervened not wanting Amelia to lose her friendship over Damon's secrets.

For the rest of the time, we sat in silence. Paying our bill, we were out the door. Leaving the shop Amelia was pissed. Walking back to the car she stopped.

"Kim, I'm telling you; these hoes will try you every time. As much as I hang out with my husband, I have never seen her around. You and I both know Bump knows everybody Damon knows!" Amelia continued.

"Let it go Amelia. Whatever Damon is doing or whomever he's doing will eventually come out. Calm down before you tear this car up," I told Amelia as she sped out the parking lot. "By the way you react when females show out, I take it you and Bump had some previous issues." I said curiously.

"We have but we'll save that for another time." Amelia calmed down and turned up Reflection by Money bag.

"Seriously Kim, you need to have a talk with Damon. You don't want to be blindsided by anything." Amelia said with a caring look in her eyes.

After the thirty-minute ride, we pulled in my driveway. I was just as amazed as I was this morning looking at my beautiful home.

"Thanks Amelia I'm going to go in prayer and wait for the Lord to reveal whatever Damon has going on."

Amelia and I hugged and exited the car. Unlocking the door, I opened the door taking my shoes off and carrying them in my hand. I made my way through the house again. I was so excited about decorating my office and adding an additional bookshelf. These children are about to hate me, I thought to myself. I laughed while imagining their responses. Then, the same text came to the phone **317-555-9878: He's mine now!**

I was not trying to deal this right now. I went to kitchen to start dinner. I preheated my air fryer while my ground beef browned and boiled my noodles. Forty-five minutes later, the food was done. Damon had not arrived home. I made our plates and put the rest way. I took a long hot shower and by the time I was finished, Damon came in the house with an attitude.

"What's wrong with you?" I asked while putting on my pajamas.

"Everything is good," he said not sounding too sure while emptying his pockets.

Instead of getting in a disagreement, I left him to his lie.

"The food is ready. Do you want to eat up here or downstairs?" I asked waiting on him to respond.

Warming I food up, I sat the plates on the table, then brought out bottles of water. Damon finally made it downstairs looking drained.

"What is going on with you?" I asked with my face scrunched up.

"Earlier you were upbeat and happy. Now you look drained. I'm not going to keep pressing you, but you need to discuss whatever the problem is. Is it your parents?"

"No, it's not my parents, it's a business matter. One of the permits didn't go through so I had to push the open date back," he said looking at his phone.

"This is good," he said after swallowing his food.

"Thank you," I said side eyeing him. Finishing our food, we cleaned the kitchen up went to bed.

Chapter Seven

Damon

Waking up the next morning, I was well rested. Kim was cooking breakfast and I could smell bacon frying. After moving everything from two house I was tired. It's Sunday, the kids will be home sometime today. I have been doing my best to push this Keisha situation to side. After that stunt she pulled yesterday I made a personal appearance to her house. Keisha face was priceless when she opened the door seeing me there. She looked as if she would urinate on herself. I guess she forgot who I was. Since being with Kim, I calmed down a little bit, but I will not hesitate to prove my point.

Coming out the bathroom with the towel around my waist, I looked around my room. I was blessed. I should have gotten a larger house sooner. The view from the bedroom window had me in a good head space. I was able to overlook the neighborhood. Kim seemed happier and that's all that mattered to me. I could see the sadness in her eyes the last day we were at the old house. Kim deserved better than what I was doing to her. "Damon breakfast is ready," Kim called from the bedroom door.

Going downstairs, I met Kim coming up with breakfast trays. I grabbed one, then turned around to head up the stairs following behind Kim. Kim turned the fireplace on, and we sat in front of the fireplace and ate.

"What do you have planned for the day?" I asked Kim.

"I need to get a pregnancy test. I missed two cycles. I thought it was stress but two missed cycles is more than stress."

I froze the moment she said pregnancy test. Two babies. My eyes widened at thought of the chaos that was bound to take place.

"Don't start Damon," Kim said in a frustrated voice.

"That's cool. I am in shock." I voiced.

"What time will the children be home?" I asked.

"Between four and five," Kim said getting up off the floor.

I quickly got up to help her. I grabbed the trays and took them downstairs to clean the kitchen. It was chilly outside. I told Kim to relax for a while and I would pick her test up. Hitting the remote starter on the car, I threw on a pair of jogging pants black long-sleeved shirt, back Timberlands, and a coat.

Walking to my truck I noticed how small Kim's truck had become since Daphne and David comes over more. Pulling into CVS parking lot, I parked my truck went inside, and found the pregnancy test. Being confused about which one to choose, I picked the one with the least number of boxes left on the shelf paid for it and left. Deciding to finish my Christmas gifts, I pulled into the BMW lot to get Kim a new truck. Just as I finished the deal, Keisha called.

"Damon, I decided to move to San Diego in a couple of months. However, I need for us to be on the same page when it comes to raising our child."

"Keisha. Stop playing with me about this child. Once the DNA test shows your child is mine, we can talk. Before that we don't have anything to talk about. One more thing, don't step a foot in my pizza shop, understood? Have a nice life in San Diego." I disconnected the call.

Making it back home, I ran into house trying to escape the cold weather. I removed my boots at the front door. I called Kim on the phone to see if wanted anything from the kitchen before I made my way upstairs.

"What took you so long? I thought you were going to buy the test and come right back." Kim said walking to towards me grabbing the bag out my hand.

"I had to stop by the pizza shop." I had to come up something so I would mess up Kim's surprise.

"Damon come here. I can't look at it!" Kim called jumping up and down.

I walked in the restroom, looked on the stick. She walked back in the room sitting down on the bed.

"It's official two blues lines. You are pregnant!"

She stood up with a smile on her face.

"That explains the sexy feeling all of a sudden," Kim explained.

"I noticed how good you looked in the jumpsuit," I said walking up to her kissing her luscious lips then laying her back on the bed.

After hours of making up for lost time, we fell asleep. Waking up to a ringing phone, I grabbed it to avoid waking Kim up. She was sleeping so peacefully. I walked downstairs to the kitchen to make a snack.

"Yeah," I answered seeing it was Keisha.

"I would like for you to go to the first appointment with me."

"Don't call my number no more until you are ready for a DNA test. What part of this are you not getting?" I asked her while getting frustrated.

"Damon, this is not fair. You get to move on with your life while I have to miss clients to make sure our baby is healthy while you are playhouse with a bitch you been cheating on since day one. Everybody knows you cheating except her gullible ass. You need to tell her the truth before I gather all your secrets," she said crying.

I disconnected the call. Fumbling around in the kitchen she made me lose my train of thought.

"Fuck." I yelled!

Wednesday morning came. We did our usually routine. After dropping the kids off at school, Kim and I headed to her first doctor's appointment. She found out she was six weeks pregnant. Being excited, we started discussing baby names. We decided to go grocery shopping after the appointment. I pulled into Walmart. Going to help Kim out the truck, she picked up snow and threw it in my face laughing. I laughed.

"I want to slam your butt in the snow. You won't always be pregnant."

We laughed walking inside the store. Kim grabbed a cart. We strolled the aisles slowly picking out food while cracking jokes at each other. Wandering to the baby section, I couldn't wait until it was time to shop the baby. Checking out we bumped into a woman. I stared at the woman for what seemed like hours. Suddenly our gaze broke, and I watched her get in a car and jotted down the license plate number.

Chapter Eight

Keisha

I am so tired of being in the background when it comes to Kim. Truth be told, I loved Damon. When Kim left, I went running to his house every time he called. The hold he had on me I thought was gone had come back. Before I could stop myself, my body ran to him like a rope tied around me while he pulled me towards him. Now that they have made amends, he is trying to put me to the side. Not Keisha. I will never be pushed to the side. Pulling out my phone and texting **Kim: He's mine now.** I waited for a response but never got one.

"Keisha, Keisha" Lisa yelled walking into the house.

"In here!" I yelled.

"Is Damon married?" she asked standing in the doorway with her hand on her hip. "Do not lie," she added before I could speak.

"Y…Yes." I responded looking at my phone still waiting on a response.

"I met his wife today she a sweet person." She said before turning to walk away. "I am glad you left him alone," she said with enthusiasm sitting down on my bed.

When I didn't respond she stopped talking then turned to look at me.

"You did leave him alone, right?" She questioned raising her voice.

"Why should I have left him? I met him before Kim. I have been rolling with him for as long as she has. So, no I will not leave him alone. Kim does not know how to care for man like him. He is mine and I will do anything to keep him. I bet Kim does not know Damon had sex with me while he was in San Diego," I said in a matter-of-fact manner.

"You did what?" Lisa said getting up from my bed with disappointment written on her face.

"You heard me correctly. Damon was in San Diego in attendance at the same business meeting as me. We stayed at the same hotel. Besides that, Damon and I never completely stop having sex."

By this time, Lisa's mouth was wide open. I saw sadness begin to take over. She left out my room not speaking to me for the rest of the day. I could only imagine how she would react when I tell her I am pregnant. I hate bitches like Kim. She acts as if nothing bothers her. She has been looking at all my messages leaving me on read. I called

Chains but he didn't answer. Calling it a night I went to sleep.

I woke up running to toilet vomiting. Lisa ran in my room.

"Are you okay?" She ask concerned pulling my hair out my face.

"I'm pregnant okay, I'm PREGNANT," I cried."

"Have you told Chains?" she asked.

"NO, I told Damon, but he doesn't seem concerned."

"Are you sure it's Damon's?"

"Yes, I'm sure, it's his," I responded sarcastically, not sure who the father is.

Lisa helped me out the bathroom and put me back in the bed. Leaving me to my thoughts, she walked out and closed the door. Pulling myself together, I called Chains and he answered on the first ring.

"Hey babe!" he said.

"Hey, I miss you. When can I see you?"

"You know Christmas is coming up so it will have to be after Christmas. How about you come here for a couple days? I miss you too!" He smiled through the phone.

"Chains I'm pregnant," I cried.

"Stop crying. I'll fly you out in a couple of days so we can discuss this in person. I'll talk to you tomorrow with all the details," Chains said then ended the call.

After showering, I opened my closet door to figure out my outfit for the day. I chose a navy-blue pencil skirt nude blouse, navy blue jacket, and nude heels. I grabbed my briefcase, then headed towards the door. I opened the door and seeing Damon, I caught my breathe.

"This is not a social call. I know you are texting Kim's phone. Don't text her anymore. I'll be there to support my child IF it is mine but leave my wife out of it. I told you from the beginning I was not leaving my wife. Now here you are pregnant and guess what I AM NOT LEAVING MY WIFE FOR YOU. Stop coming to my house uninvited," he said through gritted teeth.

"You will do whatever I tell you to do," I started to go in on him. He totally disregarded anything I was saying. He got in his car and drove off.

Doing exactly what he said, Chains called giving me my flight information. After meeting with my clients for the day, I started packing getting excited about seeing Chains. Unlike Damon, he was more concerned about the well-being of his child.

The day came for me to board my flight to San Diego. Walking to the boarding area I started to get queasy. I rushed to restroom cutting the line. Making it just in time, I let loose in the toilet until I was dry heaving. I walked out the stall then over to sink to rinse my mouth then placed some mints in my mouth. Walking out the restroom people were staring and rolling their eyes. Paying them no attention, I swung my hair side to side. Taking a seat, waiting on my flight to be called, I scrolled Facebook and seeing Kim having a Facebook piqued my interest. I clicked on her page, and it was private. Bitch!

Arriving in San Diego, the weather was gorgeous! The sun was shining. My man rolled up in a Porsche Cayenne 2020 SUV.

"Hi baby!" I ran to jump in his arms.

 He hugged me so tight and kissed my lips.

"I missed you so much."

"I missed you too!" He smiled.

He put me down, then we walked to the truck. He opened the door and I hopped in. He placed my luggage in the back.

"I got you a house to stay in while you visit. I won't have my baby staying in a hotel and stranded." He said as we held hands while he drove.

"Will you be able to stay with us today?"

"Not today but soon. I got your doctor's appointment set up." He said taking a glance at me.

Instead of answering my mind went to Damon. I been chasing this fool around thinking I would be the one he keeps around. Feeling naive I didn't respond.

"Keisha. Keisha!" He yelled and shook my hand to get my attention.

"I was taking in the sites as we drove by. It's so beautiful here, maybe I could make this my home."

"I am glad you said that. I don't want to be away from my child." Chains said driving through a well-established community.

He pulled in the driveway. It was a nice ranch style home. We walked into a fully furnished house. I was impressed.

"You know my style," I said walking through the house smiling.

I had Victorian furniture in the living room with white walls. Four-bedrooms with a large sitting area in the master room. In the garage sat a Lexus RX. By the time I came in the house, Chains had brought in my luggage and placed them in one of the bedrooms. Chains kissed me giving me the keys to the house and truck.

Chapter Nine

Kim
December

Christmas was two weeks away. Damon took the boys to purchase a tree. The girls and I stayed behind to sort through the ornaments. Looking at the homemade ornaments the children made in their younger years made me realize how far Damon and I had come.

"We should purchase larger bubs for the tree. If I know dad, he will purchase the largest tree there. Adding small bubs will be an insult." I agree Onya added.

"Let's see what the tree looks like first. I don't want to go out in ten-degree weather if I don't have to."

I told the girls living the room go to check on my homemade chicken noodle soup.

Onya's phone buzzed indicating a message had come in. Ignoring her phone after she looked had me questioning her.

"Onya are you going to answer your phone?"

"No" she said.

"I told goofy I was done."

Daphne spit her drinking out her mouth laughing hysterically. "I'm sorry," she said covering her mouth walking to the sick to wash her hands.

"Who is goofy?" I inquired. She looked at me like I knew who she was referring to.

"Mrs. Kim," Daphne said dramatically looking me.

"Goofy (Lizard) is the guy she liked until she found he has a baby on the way." Daphne spilled all the tea.

Onya high fived Daphne. "Better her than me," Onya said picking up her phone blocking him.

I turned around. "Onya are you having sex?" I asked with my hand on my hip.

"NO." she yelled while laughing. Daphne shook her head. "Mrs. Kim you are something else" in Kevin Hart's voice. "You two are something else. Now set the table." I spoke.

Hearing the front door chime. We walked to the front door. Hearing Daniel tell Jr. to move I shook my head.

"Daniel, move out the way. David, turn your body to the left." Damon gave instructions as they struggled to get the tree in the house do the wideness of the tree.

Making their way inside the house they placed in front of the bow window. It was just like Daphne said large and wide.

"Well girls, I guess we will be going shopping for ornaments tomorrow," I said packing the ornaments way.

"Dinner is done. Go wash your hands and I will start fixing the plates."

I walked in the kitchen to start fixing plates. After dinner everyone went to their rooms. I decided to sit downstairs in the front window to look at the snow falling. Looking out the window I got caught up in my thoughts. Yawning I went upstairs. Damon had already showered and snoring. I followed right behind him.

Waking up later than usually, Daniel was sitting at the nook eating cereal talking to Daphne.

"Daddy left to take David and Jr. to school," Daphne informed me.

"You two go get ready, so I can take you all to school."

An hour later we were out the door. My truck seemed to be shrinking. We drove out the driveway headed back to city. Dropping everyone off I made it to work after 9 am.

"You decided to come to work today?" He said looking me up down trying to be discreet. Just as he walked towards me the door opened.

In walked a brown skin woman wearing a long mink coat with straight black hair.

"Damon may a have a moment of your time in private." She asked.

"Whatever you have to discuss with him you can tell him in front of me." I said looking between the two of them."

"No disrespect, she said with a smirk on her face. I thought you were an employee."

Before I could say anything, Damon intervened. "What is that you want to discuss?" He asked becoming frustrated.

"I just wanted to let you know in person the renovations are done. We are waiting for the final inspection then you can move in," the woman said.

"Thank you for delivering the news. Chains could have called," he said then opened the door giving her the hint to leave.

"No, problem I love to give messages in person. Chains was busy handling some other matters and I was in the area and decided to stop by."

"Well, don't make it a habit," I said giving her a smile, but it quickly vanished.

Rolling her eyes. She turned on her heels then left.

"Damon who was that? She looks familiar?" I asked walking to my office.

"That was Chain's assistance/realtor." He quickly said then changing the subject.

"How much more shopping is there to be done?" As we walked to my office.

I put my purse on my desk. The only thing I have left to purchase are the ornaments for the tree. The girls and I will wrap the boys' things this weekend.

"Being that Christmas is around the corner. I can have it set up so you can work from home." Damon said.

Shooting him a don't try me look. Damon walked up behind me wrapping his arms around my waist.

"You are getting farther along in your pregnancy, and I don't want you under a lot of stress. Not only that, it's icy outside, and I would not want you to hurt yourself."

"Ummm-humm. I'll take you up on that offer. I am getting tired of being in the cold," I said turning around kissing him.

Chapter Ten

Damon

I contacted a private investigator friend of mine. He was able to determine the woman at Walmart was my mother. I sent some of people to watch her to make sure everything was on the up and up. Everything was good for me to approach her. One morning I decided to make the drive. I pulled into middle class neighborhood. She lived in small house with an attached garage. I could tell her bushes had been pulled up due to the change in seasons. I got out the car walked up to house and ring the doorbell. A heavy-set dude came to the door.

"Can I help you?"

"I am looking for Heaven Anderson."

A woman came from behind the door with brown skin and white hair brushed straight back that stopped at her shoulders.

"Damon," she said and covered her mouth. Tears ran from her eyes non-stop.

"Momma."

I pushed passed by the dude grabbed my mom then hugged her so tight. I didn't want to let go.

"Come in."

She pulled me inside then closed the door behind me. Not knowing where to begin. She offered me something to drink. I politely declined. She introduced me to Edward. He helped to hospital after being spotted walking to hospital. He stayed around to help me get better. I didn't have any family members to contact. Your father never responded to the calls or messages that were left on his voicemail. I sat with her for about three hours. Not wanting to leave but I had process everything she was saying. We exchanged numbers I told her I would be back and I would like for her to meet my family.

The drive home was quiet. I called my sister Denise.

"Hey Damon!" she answered with music blasting in the background.

"Hey Denise!" I know Kim already ask but are you all coming for Christmas?" I asked solemnly.

"I was trying to surprise you but Yes well be there." 'Good, I have a surprise for you. Love you talk to you later." Disconnected my call and continue to drive in silence.

Making it back to Kim. I heard Jr., David and Daniel in the kitchen plotting to prank on Daphne.

"When she smacks y'all. You better not hit her back."

I heard Kim say from the pantry.

"Hey woman! What are you doing?"

"Getting dinner prepared." She said with a hand full of items.

Attempting to help her she turned her elbow blocking me from taking anything out her hand. She made to the island and placed everything down at one time. Looking at my watch, I noticed the kids were home early.

"I picked them up early to avoid the snow that's coming later today," Kim told me.

"You look tired go lay down. The kids and I will finish cooking."

"Thank you, for some reason I am feeling tired," Kim responded.

I walked Kim up to bed then made her a sandwich with fruit on the side. Unbeknownst to Kim, I called her doctor to have someone make a house call asap.

Two hours later Dr. Franks was at the door.

"I appreciate you coming out in this weather," I told him leading the way upstairs to Kim. Kim was sitting up in the bed laughing at the tv. Seeing us, she turned the tv off. Introducing Dr. Franks to Kim, he told us what he was going to do. He started with her temperature, then her vital signs. Her blood pressure was a little higher than normal. He drew some blood saying the results will be back in a couple days. Going over a few more precautions, he was done. Walking Dr. Franks out the door, I got the kids situated for the evening then hurried to get back with Kim.

"That was nice of you to call the doctor over. Kim stated leaning over giving me a kiss.

"I don't want you bleeding or having any complications. I need to talk to you about something."

"What is it?"

"I found my mom. Remember the lady I was s….

"Yeah, I remember." Kim said cutting me off while listening intently.

"I made the decision to visit her today."

"How did it go?"

"It went well. My dad left her there to die. She thought Denise and I died in the house fire. I was thinking about having her over for dinner."

"That will be good."

"I can't wait to meet her," Kim said as she wrapped her arms around my neck and hugged me.

"Denise and Anthony are coming in town."

"I know I called her. She told me she was trying to surprise me. I know whose idea that was."

Kim started laughing and turned the tv on so she could finish the show she was watching before the doctor arrived. I could tell it was going to be a great night.

Kim

The next day Amelia, and I went shopping to gifts for Damon's mother.

"I wonder what it would be like having a mother in-law. I pray she isn't meddlesome," I told Amelia as we walked through Saks.

"My mother in-law and I have a wonderful relationship. She tells me to get in Bumps' butt when he messes up. The love we share is sweet. We have fun together, but we also respect each other."

After walking around for hours, I chose to purchase a day at the spa. Leaving the mall, I helped Amelia carry her bags. We laughed until we bumped into Lisa and her friend.

"Hey ladies," Lisa said.

"Hi," we said and kept walking.

Lisa's friend snickered. Amelia stopped then turned around. "Did you say something?" Amelia asked.

Lisa stopped and turned to face us. "No, Amelia she didn't. We were laughing."

"Stop, sparing these bitches feelings. Yes, we were. You bitches walking around thinking you better than everybody else," pointing her finger between Amelia and me. "We are fucking both yawl's husbands," her friend chimed in.

"Tell us more," I said as I walked up closer.

"Damon and Bump, yep. They be getting it and good."

Before any other words could be exchanged, we were going blow for blow. Security came to break the fight up. Lucky for us one of the security guards knew Damon and Bump and let us go. Amelia and I were both mad. We cussed Damon and Bump out all the way home.

When Amelia took me home, Damon's truck was parked outside. I ran through house looking for Damon and found him chilling in his mancave. I threw a pillow at him.

"What was that smart mess you were on the phone saying?" I asked standing in front of him. "I should have my pregnant ass in the house? Is that what you said? One of your disrespectful bitches told me she was fucking you. Really? Is that all you have to say?" I said smacking the back of his head as I walked up the steps.

He grabbed my arm and turned to face me with dark eyes, "Don't touch me again. You are an easy target. That's why people play with you."

"Let go of my arm." I snatched it away.

Not one time did he say she lied. Making the kids dinner, I heard the door chime indicating someone was leaving. Later that evening while lying in bed, I felt cramps.

"Damon."

I called his name, but he never answered. I rolled over to see he wasn't there. I woke Daphne up to tell her I was going to the hospital. On my way out the door, Damon pulled up.

"What's the matter with you?"

"I started cramping so I am going to the hospital."

"Get in the truck I'll take you," Damon said helping me in the truck.

Not making a fuss, I allowed him to take me the hospital. Pulling to the emergency entrance, Damon walked me to the door. They took me straight back. They hooked me up to machines and connected the baby to the monitor. The heartbeat was strong. After the waiting game, I was released and placed on bed rest until further notice. The ride home was quiet except for Charlie Wilson's *Turn off the Lights* which I didn't mind at all.

Making it back home at one am, I let know Daphne I was back. Going to my bathroom, I took a shower and Damon attempted to get in.

"Leave me alone Damon."

He got inside trying to explain. Blocking his words, I washed, rinsed, and exited leaving him talking to himself. Sitting up in the bed, I grabbed the remote. I turned on the tv getting comfortable in my bed. He turned the lights down to dim. Rubbing my stomach, he started talking.

"Kim, I don't know who the woman was, but I'll find out. I have not had sex with anyone since we've been married. I don't want you in the streets fighting. That's not lady like."

Laughing out loud, I looked at him then turned the tv up.

"I will not be disrespected in my house," he said with an attitude.

"Leave then. You heard the doctor tell me to stay stress free and on bed rest. I am really trying not cuss you out. Leave me alone until this baby comes. Go to your girlfriend's house and get out my face."

He moved his hand off my stomach and laid his hands behind his head in silence.

Chapter Eleven

Christmas Eve

Christmas Eve was here. Anthony and Denise arrived late last night. The girls came in from San Diego making Daniel happiest little boy ever. He would normally cling to Daphne and Onya now he went between the five of them. Everyone got up and dressed for the day. I took Anthony and the boys with me for the day. The girls stayed to help Kim around the house.

Gathering everyone in the Tahoe, I made an announcement. "I have a surprise for you all." All the chatter stopped.

"We are going to get my mother. My first time meeting her was about one week ago."

Anthony slowly turned his head to look at me.

"Denise thought she died in a house fire." He announced.

"She thought the same about us," I responded.

"We lost contact when I was a young boy."

By the time I talked about the past we pulled into her driveway. Parking the Tahoe, everyone was speechless. Except Daniel.

"I want get out and sit on her swing."

"Let's go."

Everyone got out. Daniel ran to sit on in her swing. I knocked on the door. She swung the door open. I was surprised to see her dressed in a pair of Christmas leggings and a long red Christmas t-shirt with a pair of fuzzy boots. Giving her a hug one by one, we walked in. I introduced her to everyone. We talked for a bit then headed back to the truck.

"Damon this is a nice truck son."

"Thank you, momma."

I looked over at her and tears ran down her face.

"You aren't one of the hot boys? Is that what they call them? Are you?" She cracked up.

I laughed it to off to avoid answering the question.

"If you don't mind, could we stop by the store I want to pick up something?"

"I don't mind at all."

Pulling into Walmart, I parked the truck. We got ready to get out.

"I can go in by myself," she disclosed.

"You can but you're not, David and Jr. go in the store with your grandmother," I told them. The boys did as they were told and exited the truck.

"I have never had bodyguards," she said looking at David and Jr. cracking up.

"Grandma they know how to fight. Jr... be quiet Daniel."

I had to stop him before she thinks I was raising some wild boys. She cracked up laughing closing the door behind her. Coming out the store she had each boy carrying two poinsettias. They helped her inside the truck. We headed home.

My phone was going off. Seeing it was Keisha, I put it on silence. Damn, I thought she was going to be a happy family with Chains. Now, she is back to make my life a leaving hell. Driving through my neighbor. My mother went on and on about how nice the homes were here. Pulling into my driveway she complemented me on the house. Getting out the car we went inside. We filed inside the house.

Just as we sat the table Damon walked in.

"Denise," he yelled with excitement.

"Why are you yelling?"

Denise's voiced faded away when she saw her mother. Momma! Denise slowly walked to her mother with tears in her eyes. They hugged. I grabbed the children and hugged them. Not a dry eye was in the house except for some of the children. I introduced everyone to our mother.

Everyone retreated to kitchen to have breakfast. After breakfast, we sat in the family room to get to know each other.

Allowing us to have some private time Kim and the children went down to the theatre room to watch Jingo Jango. Daniel hopped on Kim's lap. A couple of hours later, I called them back upstairs. We continued to get acquainted.

I helped Kim clean the dinner dishes.

"Do you think I should invite momma to spend the night with us?" I asked in big kid fashion.

"I think she would like that." Kim told me with confidence.

Walking in the family room, I decided to just come right out and ask her. "Momma do want to spend the night with us?" I asked.

"Have you lost your mind? I'm sitting here now praying them boys don't come put us in hand cuffs."

We cracked up laughing. I dropped my head.

"Gotcha! I'm playing I would love to spend time around my family."

"Now I see where Denise and Damon get their humor from," Kim said laughing.

Denise, Kim, and the girls can take you shopping for whatever you need. I handed Kim some cash and they all headed out the door.

Kim

I drove to Greenwood mall. Finding parking wasn't as bad as I thought it would be. Okay ladies, you can shop on your own. But stay together. First, whose phone has a full battery? No one answered. Stay with us. I don't have time to look around for you all. Walking through the mall, somebody wanted to stop at every store we passed by but never purchased anything. We got to Macy's and stayed in there the longest. Momma Heaven had the best time.

"We should do Christmas in matching pajamas!" She stated going through all the pajamas asking the girls what size they need. All the girls looked at me.

"How about we have a pajama party in Daphne and Onya room since you will be sleeping in their room."

"Bam" Denise and I fisted bumped making the girls laugh.

"I don't allow the children to walk around in pajamas all day." I explained to Momma Heaven.

"They have plenty of comfortable clothes to lounge around the house."

"Everyone can pick an outfit for tomorrow. Top and bottom only. No accessories," I told the girls putting a smile on their faces.

"I know my girls. They would have several different pieces of jewelry, purses, shoes, scarfs hats and whatever else they could get," said Denise.

Leaving everyone, I had to pick the boys something out. Which reminded me to pick up Damon's Christmas gift on the way home.

Five hours later we were back in the truck headed home. Surprisingly, Damon and the guys had cooked dinner. Then started Christmas Dinner. Well ladies what time will the sleep over start?

"We need cookies!" Momma Heaven said.

"Liquor" Denise yelled.

Allowing the men to make room in the kitchen we made a variety of cookies. Denise had shots of Hennessy which sent her to bed missing the sleep over. Everyone showered then met in Momma Heaven's room. The girls needed to bond with their grandmother, so I eased out the room. Making it to my room unnoticed. My eyes closed before I hit the bed.

Chapter Twelve

Christmas Day

"Momma, Daddy!" Daniel came running in our room.

"Daniel, I told you to knock on the door first. Don't just open a door. You knock first. Do you understand me?"

"Yes, sir! Can we open our gifts?" He asked with wide eyes excitedly.

Give me and your minute mother to get dressed.

"What time is it?" Kim asked.

"6:15. Tell Daniel to wait until seven."

Leaving out the room I heard laughter coming from downstairs.

"Everyone is up but us!" I told Kim laughing.

Kim pulled the covers over her head.

"Get up I got something you are going to love."

"Okay." I responded.

Removing the covers, I went to shower. Now that I am showing, I started buy maternity clothes. I picked out a red sweater, black leggings. I placed some ice on my wrist. It was Christmas Day. The way Damon and I have been going at it, I would not be surprised if he didn't buy me anything. Damon followed suit but dressed in a pair black jeans and red sweater. I see you, trying to match my fly.

Making my bed, I heard my phone message indicator go off. Seeing it was the same number, I ignored it. Boiling on the inside, I did not get up this early to be bothered with Damon's foolishness. Today was all about my children. Walking down the stairs, the Bluetooth was playing Donnie Hathaway *This Christmas.* Making to the bottom of the steps, I yelled Merry Christmas. I mustered up enough strength for the children to keep their excitement and enough strength not to cut Damon's heart out and give him a new heart. Everyone yelled back sitting around the tree waiting for us to open their gifts.

Damon and I passed all the gifts out. His face was speechless when I didn't hand him anything. I threw him that knowing look.

"I'll give you yours upstairs," I said getting off the floor.

"I can tell by the way you said that he doesn't want it." Anthony yelled making all the adults laugh. Denise hit his arm.

"Well, he doesn't. Did you hear how she said that? You might want to keep him away from her. She might kill him,"

121

Anthony said with a straight face trying to whisper but we all heard it and laughed some more.

Damon placed my coat around my shoulders.

"I will not be going anywhere this time," I yelled removing the coat from around my shoulders.

"Put the coat on," Denise hollered out with a smile on her face.

I put the coat on and walked to the front door. Damon handed me box before he opened the door. I opened the box. My face lit up. He opened the door. It was a BMW sitting outside with a bow around it.

"Hold my hand its icy." Damon demanded.

Looking at him like he was crazy, I grabbed a hold of Damon's hand. I opened the door. The red leather seats with Kim stitched in the headrest did for me. Damon opened the back door. I stuck my head inside and noticed it was three rows.

"Thank you. This was truly kind of you since our family is growing."

Closing the truck door, we made our way back inside. I gave him a hug and kiss on the cheek. Standing in front of the fireplace I rubbed my hands together.

"Okay, let's get the trash up off the floor. Then go put all your things away." Damon said in an authoritative voice.

Everyone got up to move around.

"Kim, come here."

Damon pulled me into the restroom.

"What is wrong with you?" He asked as if he really didn't know.

"Your bitches keep playing on my phone. I'm doing my best not to mess Christmas up for the kids." I said trying to keep my tears from falling from my eyes. "All you had to do was say you were seeing someone."

"I'm not, I have been telling you that for the longest, but you would rather believe a stranger over me.

"You are correct. I don't believe you. No one in their right mind would say some mess like that in the middle of a mall full of strangers. You better hope it is a lie because if not I will divorce you without blinking an eye. Now let me out this bathroom before we start fighting." I said through gritted teeth.

Pushing my way out the restroom, I went to kitchen to ask the ladies to excuse me for a moment I needed to get myself together.

Laying on my chaise in my bedroom alone is not what I had in mind on Christmas Day. But here I am imagining what it would have been like had I not accepted this house. My day would be filled with laughter and cheer. Or quietness because the children would be with Damon. Either way, I am sitting in my sorrows yet again behind Damon's mess. Hearing Damon come in caused me to sit up. I don't know what he had in mind, but I would mess him up if he tried anything.

"Can I have my Christmas gift now?" he asked.

"I gave it to you in the bathroom downstairs." I said rolling my eyes.

"I guess Anthony was right. I want my real gift." He said causing me to laugh.

"No, that's for a faithful husband not a cheating husband."

He walked up to me. I stood to my feet. We stared at each other until he retreated to the restroom. I walked into my closet looking in the mirror. I fixed myself say a prayer for whatever he's trying to hide to be exposed. I picked his gift up. Laid it on bed and left out the room to enjoy my family.

Later that evening I decided to call the number back.

"Hello!" A woman answered.

Is there something I can help with?

"You have been texting my phone with the same message. Who are you referring to?" I asked in a professional manner.

"Your husband. I know all about you KIM. Damon and I have been in a relationship for a while now." She voiced attempting to get under my skin.

Although I wanted to beat Damon's ass, I never let her know.

"Thanks for telling me that. You could have sent that in a text message instead of the mess you've sending. Have a wonderful day," I disconnected the call then blocked her.

The next day Denise, Amelia, and I went looking for gowns for Bump's appreciation party. Amelia was a little heated about the situation. Telling Denise about Damon and Bumps friend she knew exactly who were speaking about.

"Damon and Keisha messed around for years. They were never exclusive." She told us not wanting to get involved.

"Bump used to kick it with Lisa until you shut it down."

"That's the hoe he thought he was going to see until I popped up at the spot unannounced. She left out the back door before I could get a look at her. I never knew who she was, but she knew me. She was my nail tech up until now. I knew she was hiding something. Talking about she is a mutual friend of Damon's," Denise's eyes widen.

"Bump was telling the truth. He said he messed with her back in the day." I didn't believe him. Amelia said feeling bad.

"Damon walking around like he hasn't done anything. He should tell the truth and get it off his chest. Like I said before I will let this mess come out."

"The doctors put me own bed rest. I shouldn't have to deal with his mess while I am pregnant. I am doing my best to keep stress down." I spoke.

"Pregnant!" They both yelled.

"With so much going on. I haven't had time to tell the children. I need to do that." I thought out loud.

"Yes, I found out right after we moved in the house. Damon knows, so he's trying to keep me stress free. I kept getting text messages from the same number. I called it back. It was a woman talking about her and Damon had been in a relationship for a while. Let's talk about something else. I'm getting upset."

Trying on gowns put me a different mood. Making our decisions we paid for the items and exited the store.

Chapter Thirteen

New Year Eve's

Anthony and Damon needed to make a run to store for kick back and to pick Momma Heaven up to sit with the children while we stepped out for a couple of hours. I want to be home to bring the year in with the children. The party started at nine. It was six-thirty. Waking up from a nap, I went to check on the children. The girls were playing the game with the boys.

"Have yawl ate?" I asked.

"Yes ma, am. Audrey and Onya made homemade pizzas and fries." David told me. Thanks girls. "YW" Audrey yelled.

"What is yw" I asked walking toward the children. "You're welcome" They started laughing. Shaking my head back upstairs.

I ran my bath water and lit a candle so I could relax. I dozed off. Hearing Damon coming up the steps woke me up. I washed up and dried off. I put on an after five robe. I grabbed my moisturizer and rubbed it on my waxed legs. Damon walked in with a smile on his face.

"Let me help you."

I handed him the moisturizer. He massaged my back, taking his time as he slid his hands up and down my body. He was especially interested in my gluteus. When he was finished fondling me and setting me on fire, he removed his hands and stepped backwards. I slowly walked away putting the moisturizer back in its proper place without ruining the moment. I sat down at my vanity and began to put on my make up.

"Don't put on a lot," he said removing his clothes.

"I am going for a natural look," I said adding my primer.

Looking at myself I took a selfie. Removing my gown from the bag, I grabbed the right undergarments and accessories.

"You are not wearing that costume jewelry tonight."

He pulled out a white gold simple necklace with a matching bracelet and placed the items on my neck and wrist. Instead of this moment making me happy, he cooled the fire he'd just started. I knew Damon. He didn't buy me gifts because he loved me. He was buying them to try to make me forget he lied to me yet again. He was making me made. Why could he NOT tell me the truth instead of buying expensive gifts? What is the purpose of me walking around beautiful on the outside and tore up on the in the inside? I'll be glad when the shit hit the fan.

While Damon took a shower, I went downstairs to grab the girls so they could do my hair. Their room was a nice size. An hour and half later my hair had wand curls. It was nice. They blended my makeup to make it look natural. Audrey wrapped her arms around my waist. Looking in the mirror we smiled.

"Mrs. Kim, here, put this under your tongue. I know you got some haters, look at you. Plus, you married to my dad," Aubrey said handing me a razor.

Onya was shaking her head laughing.

"Mrs. Kim don't know nothing about that," Daphne said taking the razor out my hand.

I was laughing so hard tears were coming down my face. "Thank you, Aubrey. But I will be fine. I'm going to my room to finish dressing. We're going to talk about the razor later."

The girls' hands were up making all of kind of noises.

Damon was half-way dressed when I walked into the room. He was concentrating on tying his tie but stopped for a second to compliment me on my hair. "I like that hairstyle on you."

"Thanks. The girls did it for me," I said as I stepped into my dress and zipped it up. I grabbed the Burberry perfume from the dresser and lightly sprayed my neck. I didn't want to overdo it. As if on cue, Damon walked towards me and kissed my neck. He loved the way the Burberry smelled on me. I moved away not wanting him to touch me. Damon stepped back and started brushing his hair. I was grateful he didn't start an argument. I stepped into my shoes and looked in the mirror. Damon came and stood next to me. I had to admit we looked great together even though his lifestyle was making it hard for me to want us to be together. Being satisfied with our appearance, we walked hand in hand down the stairs. As soon as we reached the bottom step, the doorbell chimed. Damon ordered food from a local restaurant so we wouldn't have to cook. He grabbed the food and yelled for the kids to come eat as we headed out the front door.

We grabbed our coats. Kim was surprised to her truck running.

"We are riding in this tonight." Damon said helping me in.

"I enjoy riding in the Tahoe." That's all.

On the ride over the guys talked while Denise and I listened.

Pulling up to Amelia home it was twice the size of mine. I feel in love with the landscape. We pulled up and a valet was there to park the truck. He opened the door. Denise and I got out. Damon and Anthony helped us in the house. The Christmas decorations was perfect. Amelia and Bump came to meet us. They took our coats for the coat check. Damon held my hand as we mingled through the lite crowd. He had a live band playing softly.

"Don't look now but trouble has arrived." Denise said turning around looking and a guy, Lisa, and her friend from the mall.

Looking at Amelia, she had already peeped it out. Bump and Amelia walked over to greet the guy. I'm sure what he said but he shook his head in understanding. They walked away but I could tell Amelia was not satisfied that they were still here.

Damon and I had grabbed some food laughing with another couple. Bump walked over to get Damon. Amelia stood by me.

"That's Chris one of Bump's best employee. Bump and I agreed they could stay if they didn't cause any problems. Damon came over to me."

"We are about to head out." He stated with his hand in the small of my back.

"Okay, grab our coats I'll stay until you come back."

Damon and Anthony walked away.

Denise and I had engaged in a conversation with some of the guest. Lisa and her friend came over.

"Hi ladies," her friend said with a smirk on her face.

"Hi. I said coming out my shoes.

"Awww shit," I heard Denise say.

"Get to the point I don't have all day," I said looking in her face.

"Let's go Keisha. Hey Denise!" Lisa said looking embarrassed.

"Hi, Lisa what's going on?" Denise asked moving in between Keisha and me.

"Here baby," Damon said handing me my coat.

"Was this bitch your baby, while you were fucking me in San Diego?" Keisha said.

Before I knew it, I started throwing blows at Keisha's face knocking her to the ground. She able to land a couple of soft punches because I was pulled off her. Standing to my feet, I raised my foot.

Damon yelled, "No, Kim she's pregnant."

I froze and the incident with Pinky played in my head. I put my foot down. I gathered my composure. Walked over to Damon.

"Do you love me? Don't answer that question. I don't want to be embarrassed no more than I already have. Just like Pinky, I was ready to have his ass locked up. But noooo. I couldn't because of shit she had hanging over your head. Now this bitch comes into my friend husband event starting shit, but I can't do her bad because she's pregnant. But did you forget I was pregnant too!?" I looked around the room. Damon was speechless. The entire place was silent. I had tears rolling down my face. Denise tried to wipe them away.

"Let my tears flow. This is a healing process for me." I told Denise with a smile on my face.

I walked in the kitchen with Damon behind me. I started throwing knives at Damn and cussing him out.

"Kim stop the police are coming."

The room had cleared out. Snatching my coat off the ground I walked to my truck got in on the driver side, but the valet had the keys. He was nowhere in sight. Bump retrieved my keys handing them to me. Once I got inside with Denise and Anthony in tow, I locked the door and drove home bumping Rihanna's *needed me.*

Making home at 11:15 pm I went upstairs to shower and cried the entire time. I dried off. I put moisturizer on my face. I threw on a pair of jogging pants and shirt, making it back downstairs in thirty minutes. I went to the kitchen to make a bowl of ice cream. I was determined to bring the new year in with my family.

"How was the party?" Daphne asks.

"Don't ask." Denise said.

"I should have taken the razor," I responded sitting on the couch with a bowl of ice cream watching the count down.

"Razor," Denise repeated.

"The girls basically told me to put a razor under my tongue for hating ass bitches."

"Kim, don't never let anyone bring you out your character."

Forgetting she was there, "I apologize Momma Heaven."

"We can talk about later," she stated.

"5,4,3,2,1 Happy New Year," we all yelled while jumping up and down hugging one another. My mood changed seeing Damon walk through the door. Ignoring him, I grabbed the sparkling grape juice opening it pouring the children some.

"Kim, can I talk to you for a minute?" Damon asked.

Tears poured down my face. Breathing in and out, I walked to our room. Damon talked and talked. Not hearing nothing he was saying, I finally climbed in my bed and fell asleep.

"Bitch, you hear me," Damon snatched the covers off me.

I pulled my forty-five from the side of the mattress and hopped up quick.

"You want talk, talk. Talk," I yelled pointing the gun at his head.

"I said I apologize."

"Apologize for…." What is that you apologize for? I asked.

"Kim, you left, I was lonely. I kept asking you to come back home."

"You kept brushing me off. Now you making a baby is my fault. Get the fuck out my house."

"This is my house, Kim. I paid for this house," Damon said really believing he was staying here.

"I will not move again. I was at home when you came to my house. I didn't call you. I even told you to find someone else. You did just that. Go be with her. Leave," I hollered!

Damon walked out. Feeling relieved I laid down and cried myself to sleep. The next morning Denise, Anthony and Momma Heaven went home. Damon had come home to see everyone off. I stayed in the theater room until it was time to say goodbye to the girls. Once they were gone, the rest of us chilled for the rest of day.

Tuesday had come. I prepared myself to file for a divorce with full custody of the children with child support. Walking into Monty's office, Lisa was there. I threw daggers at her with my eyes, but she didn't say anything to me. Monty came out.

"Hello!" He greeted with a smile.

"I was expecting to see you sooner. I thought things changed but I guess not," I said holding in my tears.

He drafted the petition for a divorce. He gave me a copy and Damon's would be mailed to him.

Months of us going back and forth about the house and the children started to drain us. Damon decided to move out. Keisha did not get the memo of Damon and I not being together. She sent me some old pictures of her them together with a full video. Sending it straight to Damon he was pissed. Oh, well!

February

Damon came by the house to check on us. Grabbing the mail. He ran across the divorce decree.

"Kim. I thought we would be slowly work on things. I have respected your wishes by totally moving out the house. I'm in counseling. I want my family. This is not what I want," he said in a defeated voice.

"It may not be what you wanted but this is what you asked for. You cheated on me, got the bitch pregnant, then had the nerve to call me a bitch when I ignored you. This all came within the two months of us moving into this house. This is exactly what you asked for. We must be cordial for the children but that other stuff is off limits. I need time to heal this was too much for me. Every time I think about it, I want to kill you for taking up for her. You go and do whatever you want without thinking of the consequences. I think I need to see a counselor myself." Cutting the conversation short, I said, "The children are in their rooms."

Damon visited with the children while I cooked dinner. He kissed me on the cheek and then he left. That had become our normal and I was fine with it.

Chapter Fourteen

Damon

Kim was in her last trimester. She had been so focused on taking care of the children and home, that she had not started on the baby's room. I told her to order anything she wanted for the baby so she would not have to go out in the bad weather. As the items came, she bossed me and the boys around to make sure everything was in the correct place. Finding out it was a girl, Kim and the girls went crazy shopping for the baby as well as themselves. Denise and Amelia gave a baby shower for family only. That only added to what Kim bought.

The last month of Kim's pregnancy she was confined to the bed until she delivered the baby. I moved in the guest room to help with the children. Along the way I moved back into the bedroom. Kim would only allow me to rub her stomach and feet. Thankfully, my baby was healthy weighing eight pounds seven ounces looking just like Kim. We named her Destiny. Once a routine was started. Once I seen the divorce was final. I decided to purchase me house. It hurt my heart the children were coming back and forth. Kim let me come by whenever to help with the kids. I guess that is all I could really hope for. Kim and I are not over by a long way. Seeing counselor helped me to see the error in my ways.

My mother has been a huge blessing to my family. She allows Kim and I took work through our problems without getting involved. I really did not expect for Kim to find out about Keisha the way she did. Bump had been warning me to come clean, but my pride would not allow me to. Now I am wifeless. My house is lifeless again and I am the only one to blame. I pray Kim will allow me another chance to make things right.

Oh, yeah the DNA test determined Keisha's baby was not mine. Since the results of the DNA test, I have not heard from Keisha and that was fine with me. Amelia and Bump are expecting their first child.

The End

A word from the author...

Although this story is fiction, there are many scenarios that end like this. We all get one life. Decide to make better choices about who you allow in your life. My father always told me to make decisions I will not regret. Not one of us is perfect so we must forgive when others have wronged us. However, we do not have to allow the same person to hurt us over and over again.

Thank you to all my supporters. Thank you for your interest in my books. I pray it helps you to pay attention to red flags before you make life changing decisions.

You can connect with me on Facebook- Author LaCinta Brown or Instagram @Authorlacintabrown